The Complete FREDDY THE PIG Series
Available or Coming Soon from the Overlook Press

FREDDY

THE COWBOY

He squirted the entire contents of the pistol into the man's face.

FREDDY

the

COWBOY

by WALTER R. BROOKS

Illustrated by Kurt Wiese

THE OVERLOOK PRESS
WOODSTOCK & NEW YORK

If you enjoyed this book, very likely you will be interested not only in the other Freddy books published in this series, but also in joining the *Friends of Freddy,* an organization of Freddy devotees.

We will be pleased to hear from any reader about our "Freddy" publishing program. You can easily contact us by logging on the either THE OVERLOOK PRESS website, or the Freddy website.

The website addresses are as follows:
THE OVERLOOK PRESS:
www.overlookpress.com

FREDDY:
www.friendsoffreddy.org

We look forward to hearing from you soon.

First published in the United States in 2002 by
The Overlook Press, Peter Mayer Publishers, Inc.
Woodstock & New York

WOODSTOCK:
One Overlook Drive
Woodstock, NY 12498
www.overlookpress.com
[for individual orders, bulk and special sales, contact our Woodstock office]

NEW YORK:
141 Wooster Street
New York, NY 10012

Dust jacket and endpaper artwork courtesy of the Lee Secrest collection and archive.

Library of Congress Cataloging-in-Publication Data

Brooks, Walter R., 1886-1958.
Freddy the Cowboy / Walter R. Brooks ; illustrated by Kurt Wiese.
p. cm.
Summary: Freddy the pig buys a horse and inadvertently makes an enemy of an unscrupulous cowboy with designs on the First Animals' Bank and on Freddy's life.
[1. Pigs—Fiction. 2. Domestic animals—Fiction. 3. Cowboys—Fiction.]
I. Title. PZ7.B7994 Frh 2001 [Fic]—dc21 2001059339

Manufactured in the United States of America
ISBN 1-58567-225-4
1 3 5 7 9 8 6 4 2

FREDDY

THE COWBOY

Chapter 1

Charles' friends rather enjoyed listening to his speeches when they didn't have anything else to do. If he was supposed to be speaking about patriotism, for instance, it was fun to see how long he could go on without really saying anything about it. But today the other animals felt that he was being a nuisance. For this meeting had been called for a purpose, and listening to this rooster wasn't getting them anywhere.

The chairman of the committee, Freddy, the

pig, was sitting in a chair propped against the
wall on the shady side of the pig pen. He would
have been more comfortable on the ground
with the others, for pigs aren't built for chairs.
Any more than chairs are built for pigs. Pigs'
legs are too short, and chairs' legs are too long.
But of course the place for a chairman is *in* a
chair, not lolling in the grass.

Eeny, one of the mice, had spoken first. Life
on the Bean farm was getting dull, and, said
Eeny: "I like excitement, adventure. What are
we going to do to make life more interesting?"

At that Charles had flown up on to the back
of Freddy's chair. "Friends and fellow Bean-
ites," he shouted, "my distinguished colleague,
Eeny, has said the word. Excitement, adventure! Those are the words. Interest, excitement,
even danger. Yes, my friends, danger. For danger is truly the spice of life." And he went on
for some time in praise of danger, with many
instances of the gay and careless manner in
which he himself had met the most terrifying
situations.

"Danger!" the rooster shouted. "I rise to
meet it with laughter on my lips."

"Ho, hum!" said Jinx, the black cat, and he

There was a squeal from Freddy and a squawk from Charles . . .

reached out and hooked a claw around the leg of Freddy's tipped-back chair and yanked hard. There was a squeal from Freddy and a squawk from Charles and a crash from the chair as they all came down together. "There you are, rooster," said the cat. "There's your catastrophe. Let's see you rise to that with a loud Ha, ha!"

Charles rose all right, and with wings spread and beak lowered he went for the cat. "You big bully!" he said. "I'll teach you to play smart-aleck jokes on me!"

But Jinx bounded off and up a tree, and stretched out along a limb above the rooster, who was dancing with rage: "What are you kicking about?" he said. "You claim you love danger and excitement, and then when I give them to you, you get mad. There's just no pleasing some folks."

Freddy had got up and was rubbing his head, which had got bumped against the wall of the pig pen. "Look here, Jinx," he said crossly, "this is a committee meeting, not a battle. You know that the thing to do is to let Charles make his speech, and when he's finished we can go on with the meeting."

"Yeah," said the cat. "Well, I can figure out plenty of kinds of excitement. But listening to a silly old rooster telling me how brave he is isn't one of them. Heck, I don't have to get a committee together; I can give you all the excitement you want. You want some, hey? OK, leave it to me." And he dropped from the limb, made a quick pass at Charles, then dodged and dashed off down towards the farmhouse.

"Well," said Freddy, when he had set up the chair again and climbed back into it, "Now that we've heard Charles, has anyone else any suggestions?"

"But I haven't finished!" the rooster protested.

"You never do finish, Charles," said Mrs. Wiggins, the cow. "The only time you stop is when your audience walks out on you. So why not let somebody else talk now?"

"You, I suppose?" said Charles sarcastically.

"Land sakes, I'm no speechifier," the cow said. "But I'd like to make a suggestion. In the first place, we don't want Jinx's kind of excitement—pulling chairs out from under people."

"If Jinx wants real excitement," said Quik,

"He might try dropping a nice squashy tomato on Mr. Bean when he comes out of the house after dinner."

The other mice giggled and nudged one another, but Freddy frowned at them, and they were just quieting down when Hank burst into a loud neighing laugh. Hank always had a hard time making up his mind about anything, and it had taken him quite a while to decide if Quik's remark was funny. But when he finally decided, he gave it all he had. He roared with laughter. "Good squashy tomato, hey?" he said. "That wouldn't be excitement, mouse, that would be murder. Cat murder. Caticide would be the word for it, hey, Freddy?"

"Yeah," said the pig, "Very funny. And now suppose we let Mrs. Wiggins finish what she started to say."

"Well," said the cow, "I was just going to say that it's sort of foolish to sit around and moan about how life is so dull, and complain that nothing ever happens. The thing to do is to go out and make things happen. And no committee is going to do that for us; we have to do it ourselves."

"You mean like when we started the First

Animal Bank?" said Freddy. "That was interesting all right. But it goes along so smoothly now that there isn't any excitement in it any more. And by the way, Eeny, you haven't paid back that ten cents you borrowed two months ago."

As President of the First Animal, Freddy had to keep track of money that was loaned out. The animals were mostly pretty honest, and paid back as soon as they could, but there were a few like Eeny who had to be reminded a good many times.

"Well, you don't need to dun me for it right in front of everybody," said Eeny crossly.

"That's the only way we can ever get some of you animals to pay up," said Freddy. "Let everybody know about it, and then you get ashamed and bring the money back. Anyway, you didn't tell the truth about what you wanted the money for. You said it was to go to the movies in Centerboro. But I've found out that you mice always get into the movie free. You get in through the hole beside the cellar window and go up through the partition into the balcony, and so you didn't need the money for a ticket."

Eeny looked scared. "Well," he stammered,

"I—I didn't think you'd let me have the m-money if I told you why I wanted it. We wanted to give Quik a birthday party and I used it to buy cheese."

"Why, of course the bank would have let you have it, Eeny," said the pig, "But—"

Mrs. Wiggins interrupted him. "Great grief, Freddy, can't you forget your old ten cents long enough to let me finish what I started to say? What have mice in the movies got to do with this meeting? I wanted to say that the way to make life more interesting isn't to sit around and growl about it, it is to go out and hunt up something. Look for adventures. Suppose we all start out in a different direction. I'll bet you that not one of us would go half a mile off the farm before something interesting would turn up."

"If it's interesting to be eaten up by a cat or a hawk, I guess you're right," said Eek. "How far do you think a mouse would get, starting out in search of adventure?"

"You don't have to go alone," said Freddy. "One of you could go with each of us. My gracious, that's a good idea, Mrs. Wiggins. Suppose we leave this afternoon, and then meet

back here in a week's time and tell our adventures. Come on, let's tell the other animals and see who wants to go."

So that afternoon quite a number of the animals came up to the pig pen, all ready for the road. And they drew lots for the direction they were to start in. Hank, with Eeny on his back, went east; Freddy and Quik went northeast; Mrs. Wiggins went north; Charles and his wife Henrietta went northwest; Jinx went west; Robert the collie, and Cousin Augustus southwest; Bill, the goat, with Eek, went south, and Georgie, the little brown dog, and Mrs. Wurzburger, one of Mrs. Wiggins' sisters, went southeast.

All the animals were in high spirits except Charles. He hadn't wanted Henrietta to go. "Who ever heard of a knight errant starting out in search of adventure and taking his wife along!" he grumbled. "You'd think I was going to a party."

"You will be if you go running around the country alone," said the hen. "Only you'll be the one on the platter, and the rest of the guests will be tucking their napkins under their chins. No, sir, either I go or you stay home. There's got to be somebody along to get you out of the scrapes you'll get into."

Mr. and Mrs. Bean stood on the back porch looking up towards the pig pen as the animals all started out. "What on earth do you suppose they're up to now?" said Mrs. Bean, "Some new game?"

Mr. Bean shook his head. He never interfered with his animals as long as they did the little jobs around the farm that he expected of them. He turned to go in and caught sight of a folded piece of paper lying near the door. He picked it up, looked at it right side up, sideways and upside down, then handed it to Mrs. Bean. "You got your specs on," he said. "What's it say?"

"Why, it's addressed to Freddy," said Mrs. Bean, "Wonder how it got here?"

Mr. Bean took his pipe out of his mouth and gave a shrill whistle. The pig pen was so far from the house that he couldn't call to the pig, so when the animals looked down towards him, he crooked his first finger and held it behind him like a tail. And as Freddy was the only animal there with a short curly tail he started down towards the house.

"That was right smart of you, Mr. B," said Mrs. Bean. "What would you have done if you'd wanted the rooster?"

Mr. Bean put the tips of his fingers together and made a beak of them, with which he pecked at the railing as if picking up corn. Then he said: "Mrs. Wiggins," and stuck his forefingers up beside his head like horns.

"Ah, but how about the mice?" said Mrs. Bean.

"Easy." He made his hand into a mouse and ran it along the railing and up a post.

Mrs. Bean laughed, and as Freddy came up she handed him the paper. "I just found this on the floor," she said. "I guess it's yours."

Mr. Bean stuck his pipe back in his mouth and went indoors. He was proud of his animals because they could talk, but it always made him nervous if he heard them.

"Goodness!" said Freddy, as he unfolded and read the paper. That was a pretty weak expression, considering what was printed on it in rather shaky capitals. "Beware!" it said. "The Horrible Ten are after you. The order for your execution has been signed. Return the jewels in ten days or it will be carried out. Get smart, fat boy. Our knives thirst for your blood.

(Signed) THE HORRIBLE TEN."

And there were ten little knives drawn at the bottom of the sheet.

"Golly!" said Freddy. Mrs. Bean had gone into the house. Most of the animals had disappeared in the directions assigned to them, but Hank was still in sight, plodding slowly eastward across the pasture, and two moving dots up towards the woods were Charles and Henrietta. There was no one to talk to about this new and terrifying development except Mrs. Wiggins' slow-witted sister, Mrs. Wogus, and she would be no help. "Golly!" said Freddy hopelessly, and went slowly back to the pig pen.

Chapter 2

Quik was waiting impatiently. He shouted to Freddy to hurry, but a mouse's voice is pretty small, and Freddy couldn't hear him until he got very close. Then he said irritably, "Oh, shut up! Haven't I got enough on my mind without you yelling at me? Look at this." And he showed the mouse the letter.

"'The Horrible Ten,'" said Quik. "Never heard of 'em." "Neither did I," said the pig.

"I suppose you could look 'em up in the

phone book," said Quik. "Whose jewels did you steal, Freddy?"

"Oh, my goodness, I didn't steal any jewels," said Freddy crossly. "I never heard of them till five minutes ago. Or of these horrible whatever-they-are's."

Quik gave a small sniff. "That's what *you* say," he said. "They seem to know you all right, though." He shook his head thoughtfully. "I don't know," he said: "Remember all the trouble you had with the Ignormus? . . . and there was only one of him. If I were you I'd give the stuff back."

"I keep telling you I haven't got any 'stuff,' " said Freddy angrily.

"Sure, sure," said the mouse soothingly. "But they think you have. In that case I'd just quietly leave the country."

"That's just what I'm going to do," Freddy said. "I mean I'm going out in search of adventure, just as we planned. Only I'm going in disguise, so if these people are after me they won't recognize me."

He had a number of disguises that he used in his detective work, and now he put on a red and green checked suit that Mr. Bean had once bought in Paris but had never had the nerve to wear. Mrs. Bean had cut it down for Freddy. It wasn't very becoming, but at least he didn't look like a pig in it. I don't know what he did look like.

So with Quik in one side pocket and the letter from the Horrible Ten in the other, he went northeast, up through the pasture and across the upper road and through a corner of the Big Woods past the Witherspoon farm. A hill and a valley and another hill, and there was Otesaraga Lake sparkling in the sunshine before them.

"Do we have to keep straight on northeast, Freddy?" Quik asked. "Because if we do we'll have some adventures with fish." He had climbed to Freddy's shoulder.

"This is the east end of the lake," said Freddy. "We'll go round it and then on. That's Mr. Camphor's big house—see?—off there to the left. I guess he'd hide us there if that gang was after us."

"What do you mean—*us?*" the mouse demanded. "It's you they're after, not me. I haven't stolen any jewels."

"Say, look, mouse," said Freddy. "How'd you

like to walk home alone, on your own four little legs?"

"Walk home?" said Quik incredulously.
"From here? Why, it would take me a couple
of days."

"That's right," said the pig. "That's what it
will take you if you don't pipe down about my
stealing things."

So Quik didn't say any more. They went on
around past the cabins at the end of the lake
and plunged into the woods, for this was the
southern edge of the Adirondack forest. It was
dark under the trees, and very still except for
the queer little rustlings and whisperings that
—well, Freddy couldn't help imagining that it
might be the Horrible Ten creeping along after him, slipping from tree to tree, grinning
and muttering and brandishing their sharp little knives.

"What you shivering for—you cold?" Quik
asked.

"Got a little chill, I guess," said Freddy.
"Coming out of the sunshine into this damp
shade."

"It doesn't bother me any," said the mouse.
"Maybe if you gave those jewels back your

teeth wouldn't chatter so much."

"Say, look," Freddy said. "I keep telling you that I don't know any more about that business than you do. I—" He stopped suddenly, for somewhere off to the right a man had started shouting angrily. "Wonder what that is?" said the pig, and turned towards the sound.

After a short distance the trees thinned, and then he was standing at the edge of an open pasture. Beyond was a long low house and, beyond that, other fields stretched for half a mile or so before the woods enclosed them again. There were barns and other buildings, and near the house a fenced-in space with a dozen horses scattered about in it. And just outside the fenced-in space—which from the Western movies he had seen Freddy knew must be a corral— a man was holding a horse by the bridle and beating him over the head with a heavy whip.

Freddy forgot all about the Horrible Ten. "Hey!" he shouted. "You quit that." And he started across the pasture.

The man paused with the whip raised and looked round. He was dressed like a cowboy, in blue jeans, boots, a bright-colored shirt and a ten-gallon hat. Freddy couldn't imagine what he was doing there, in the middle of New York State. Probably the man had just as much trouble trying to account for Freddy, for what he saw come stumbling towards him was a little man about four feet high in a suit of a plaid so bright that most people would be scared to wear even a necktie made of it.

"You quit beating that horse!" Freddy shouted again.

The man just looked at him. He didn't smile and he didn't glare angrily. He was tall and thin and sour looking, and that's really about all you can say about him. And all the times that Freddy saw him his face never changed; it had no more expression on it than a pickle.

He spoke in a low creaky drawl, as if his voice needed oiling. "What you aimin' to do about it, pardner? He's my horse."

"What are you licking him for?" Freddy asked.

"Not that it's any of your business," said the man, "But this horse is one of the meanest, orneriest critters I ever—Hey!" he shouted, and ducked as the horse jerked back on the bridle and then snapped at his arm with long vicious-looking teeth.

"Hey!—You quit that."

"Well, if he's dangerous, why don't you sell him?" Freddy asked.

The man, who had raised his arm to hit the horse again, paused. "You want to make me an offer for him?" he asked.

Freddy had quite a lot of money in the First Animal Bank. As a detective he had earned several good-sized rewards for capturing criminals wanted by the police. He could certainly afford to buy the horse, and he was willing enough to do it, to save it from being abused by a cruel owner. But if the horse really was vicious, it would be foolish to buy him.

He looked at the horse. He was small—a cow pony, Freddy supposed; a buckskin, and he had on a heavy Mexican saddle, with a rope coiled over the high horn. And just then the pony turned his head and looked Freddy right in the eye and winked.

"What do you want for him?" Freddy asked.

"Why, friend," said the man, "I could let you have him for—oh, say a hundred and fifty dollars."

The horse looked at Freddy and shook his head slightly.

"Don't be silly," Freddy said. "Why should

I pay that much for a bad-tempered horse that would probably buck me into the middle of next Thursday afternoon if I tried to ride him?"

"I'll tell you why," said the man. "There can't anybody stay on that horse for more than half a minute. You see this outfit here?" He waved a hand towards the house and the corral. "I come here this spring and opened this place as a small dude ranch. Got about twelve guests here already. Along in the summer I plan to put on a rodeo, and this here horse is one of my main attractions. I offer fifty dollars to anybody that can stay on him for ten seconds. You see, there's a lot of dude ranches in the East now, and there's any number of riders from western ranches that travel round the country picking up a little money riding or roping or doggin' steers. Some of those boys'll give me a good show when they try to ride this horse. Only, I can't handle him any more. Whenever I step into the corral he goes for me, and some day he'll get me. But he wouldn't go for you, because he don't ever try to hurt anybody but me, as long as they don't try to get on him. You could take him round to the county fairs and such and make good money off him."

"I still don't see why you want to sell him," Freddy said. "But I'm not big enough to take that whip away from you and give you a good thrashing with it, so the only way to stop you beating him is to buy him. Suppose I offer you fifty dollars?"

He glanced at the horse, who nodded approvingly.

But the man said: "That ain't any sort of an offer. I guess you ain't serious, friend. I guess . . ." The horse jerked back suddenly and this time got free. He trotted off, shaking his head and snorting, then circled round and came back and stood still watching them, just out of reach of the whip.

"Dratted critter!" said the man. "Last time he got loose I didn't catch him for three days. O K, you can have him. Where's your money?"

Freddy said he'd have to go to the bank for it, and the man said he'd drive him there and went to get his car.

When he had gone, "Take off that cap, will you?" said the horse. And when Freddy had taken it off:

"Just as I thought—a pig," he said. "That Cal is so nearsighted you could've been an alligator and he wouldn't have known it till you bit his head off. But he's too proud to wear glasses. You must be one of the animals I've just heard about, live on a farm south of here. Talking animals, folks say. Well, what's so wonderful about that?"

"Nothing," said Freddy, "Only we aren't afraid to let people know we can talk, the way most animals are."

The horse shook his head. "Talk causes too much trouble. Look at the wars and things these humans have got into, and all on account of talk. The minute that animals begin to talk a lot they'll be having wars too. Rabbits will declare war on chipmunks, and gangs of cows will ambush horses and—well, anyway, what's talking good for except to argue? And who wants to argue?"

"Maybe you're right," Freddy said. "But if I hadn't talked I couldn't have bought you. Why does he want to sell you, anyway?"

The horse grinned. "There ain't anybody can stay on me if I don't want 'em to. I played fair with Cal after he first bought me. He had a dude ranch up in Maine, and when he put on a rodeo he'd offer fifty dollars for anybody could stay on me ten seconds, and I'd throw 'em right off. But he's an awful mean man. If you do something he doesn't like, he doesn't get mad and yell at you—he just quietly hauls off and hits you with a club. Or maybe you haven't done anything. Like cats for instance. He hates cats, and whenever he sees one he'll kick it. I ain't got any special love for cats myself, but I don't kick 'em just for fun. And that's the way he treated me. So naturally I tried to kick him back.

"I thought maybe he'd sell me. But he isn't afraid of me, I'll say that for him, even though I've put a number of horseshoe marks on him in different places. And I was too useful to sell. Well, this morning a couple of riders blew in, and they were braggin' about how good they were, and Cal says there's this standing offer of $50 for anybody that can stay on me ten seconds. The dudes all came out to watch, and Cal held my head while one of the riders got into the saddle. Then he let me go, and the rider began yelling and digging me with his spurs and whacking me with his hat like they're supposed to do when they ride a bucking horse.

"But I didn't buck. I just trotted around as meek as a mouse with a headache. That boy looked awful foolish, carrying on that way. So I waited till the time was up. Then—well, then I let him have it and he landed on his nose. But he'd stayed the time, so Cal had to hand over the money.

"I did the same with the other rider. It cost Cal a hundred dollars. That's why he was beating me. And that's how I made him want to get rid of me. He isn't sure any more that I can be counted on to buck a rider off when he wants me to." He stopped and looked sharply at Freddy. "What you want to buy me for?" he asked. "I never heard of a pig buying a horse. Of course if you've really got the fifty dollars, I can tell you you're getting a real bargain."

"You're no bargain to me!" Freddy snapped. He was a kind-hearted pig, and to buy the horse had seemed the only way to stop the man from abusing him. But he was beginning to wonder if fifty dollars wasn't a good deal to spend for something he couldn't use. And he thought, too, that it would be nice if the horse seemed a little grateful. "I'm not so sure I want to buy you after all."

"Hey now, wait a minute!" said the horse. "I'm only trying to tell you that you aren't going to lose that fifty dollars. You and me can make money together, pig. Have you ever ridden horseback?"

"No, and I'm not going to try," said Freddy.

"O K, suit yourself," said the horse. "We could have a lot of fun riding around the country together and picking up a dollar here, a dollar there. I wouldn't let you fall off even if you wanted to. The folks that got thrown off horses, they haven't made friends with the horses— that's the trouble. If a stranger climbs on your back and hollers 'Giddap,' what do you do? Why naturally you bounce him off, and maybe even kick him to teach him better manners. But you and me— Hey, here comes Cal. We'll talk about this later."

The man—his name was Cal Flint—came up in his car, and Freddy got in, and they drove off, leaving the horse looking after them. Freddy kept his trotters out of sight and his cap well pulled down, and there was really nothing

to show that he was a pig but his long nose.
Mr. Flint didn't seem to notice anything. But
when they reached Centerboro and Freddy told
him to drive right on through, he looked
around curiously.

"Thought we was going to get your money
from the bank," he said.

"The Centerboro Bank isn't my bank. Mine
is on a farm a few miles west of town."

"A bank on a farm?" Mr. Flint said. "Never
heard of such a thing."

But he kept on as Freddy directed, and pretty
soon up ahead of them they saw the Bean farmhouse, and a little way before they reached the
gate Freddy told him to pull up at the right
side of the road. Then he pointed to a shed that
stood just inside the fence. "Here's the bank,"
he said.

Mr. Flint looked at the sign over the door of
the shed.

"First Animal Bank of Centerboro," he
read. "Say, who you tryin' to kid? Nobody'd
keep money in that place."

"Come on," said Freddy, and got out and
climbed the fence, and after a minute Mr. Flint
followed him.

Nowadays the First Animal was only open for business on Tuesdays, but there were always a couple of small animals on duty, guarding the trap door in the floor which was the entrance to the vaults where the money and other valuables were kept. These vaults were a series of underground chambers which had been dug by woodchucks, and added to from time to time until now, as Freddy said, you really needed a map to find your way around in them.

Freddy went in and pulled up the trap door, but as he started to get down into the hole, the edge of the door caught his cap and pulled it off. And Mr. Flint, who had been watching curiously, gave a jump. "Hey!" he said. "You—you're a pig!"

"Sure," said Freddy. "So what?"

"Me, Cal Flint," said the man as if talking to himself. "I been driving a pig around the country. I been tryin' to sell a horse to a pig!" And he broke into a sort of nervous hysterical giggle. It was the only time Freddy ever saw him laugh.

"Well," said Freddy sharply. "You want that fifty dollars or don't you?"

"You mean you got *money* down that hole?" Mr. Flint demanded.

Freddy told him to wait and then disappeared, to return in a few minutes and hand over five ten-dollar bills.

"Does the saddle go with the horse?" he asked.

"The saddle," said Mr. Flint vaguely as he tucked the money into his pocket. He acted as if he was in a daze, but Freddy saw his eyes darting inquisitively about the room, and doubted if he was as confused as he pretended. "Oh, I'll lend you the saddle and bridle till you get one of your own. But look here, pardner; is this here really a bank for animals? I mean, animals have really got money here?"

Freddy didn't like the way he watched as the trap door was lowered into place. And he particularly didn't like it when Mr. Flint's eyes caught sight of the alarm bell cord, and followed it up to where it ran through a hole in the roof. The cord was there for the guards to pull in case of burglars, and the clang of the bell would bring every animal on the farm down to the defense of the bank.

"Oh, the animals don't have much money," Freddy said. "It's just a storehouse where they can leave nuts and acorns—stuff like that—for safekeeping."

"Yeah," said Mr. Flint with a grin. "And ten-dollar bills." He went outside and walked around the shed, traced the cord up into the tree where the bell was hung, then said, "Quite a layout; yes, sir, quite a layout. Well, let's get back to the ranch. The horse is yours, only you got to catch him before you take him home."

Chapter 3

They drove back to the ranch, and the horse was standing just where they had left him. "There he is, pig, he's all yours," said Mr. Flint. Freddy got out. "You act as if you thought I couldn't catch him," he said.

"You sure read my mind," said the man, and settled back comfortably to watch the fun. But the horse never moved as Freddy walked up to him and took hold of the bridle.

Mr. Flint sat up straight. "Well, I'll be durned!" he said. "Look out there, pardner. When he's gentle as that he's plannin' trouble. You watch yourself."

"Tell him you're going to ride me home," the horse whispered.

"How can I?" the pig asked. "I'm too short to climb up into the saddle."

"Lead me over to the fence and climb on from there," said the horse.

So Freddy called to the man that he was going to ride. But when they got over to the fence, Quik, who had been sitting quietly in Freddy's pocket, climbed out and jumped over to a fence post. "Here's where I get off," he said. "So long, Freddy; let me know when you're able to have visitors and I'll drop in to see you at the hospital."

The horse turned his head and looked at the mouse. "Where'd this guy come from?" he asked. And when Freddy had explained and introduced his friend: "Pleased to meet you," he said. "Get aboard; there ain't anything to be scared of."

"Ah, who's scared!" said Quik.

"Why, I guess you are," said the horse.

"Tain't anything to be ashamed of; all rodents are timid."

"Who you calling a rodent?" Quik demanded belligerently.

"Well, you're a mouse, aren't you?" said the horse with a grin. "Or do my eyes deceive me and are you a hippopotamus?"

"Aw, quit trying to be funny!" Quik snapped. "Nobody can call me a rodent and get away with it!"

"Why it only means that you're an animal that gnaws," said Freddy. "Rats and mice are rodents, just the same as all cats are felines, and all . . ."

"What you waiting for?" Mr. Flint called. He was too shortsighted to see Quik on the fence post. "You scared of him?"

Freddy climbed up part way on the fence and flopped into the saddle. "I guess we're both scared, Quik," he said. "But it isn't anything to be ashamed of. He's promised not to bounce us off. By the way, horse, what's your name?"

"Cyclone's what they call me around here," the horse said. "Kind of silly name, ain't it? Just call me Cy."

"O K, Cy," said Freddy, taking a firm grip

of the saddle horn, "Let's go. Come on, Quik. Oh, come on! Are you a man or are you a mouse?"

This is a question which always enrages mice, because it suggests that while men are bold and fearless, mice are the most timid and cowardly creatures on earth. Of course this isn't so. Mice are small, and they keep out of the way of larger animals. No mouse would walk right up to a man, any more than a man would walk right up to an elephant or a grizzly bear. But many heroic deeds have been performed by mice. If more people knew about them they wouldn't be so scornful of these courageous little animals.

"Oh, so I'm scared, hey?" Quik shouted. He made a flying jump from the post and landed on the horse's nose, and stood there, looking straight into his eyes. "O K, you go on and do your stuff, and we'll see who sticks on longest —me or this big hunk of fat pork here." He ran up higher and made a safety belt of some of the coarse hair of the horse's forelock, which he wrapped around his middle and tied. "Go on, go on; what you waiting for?"

The horse turned his head and winked at

Freddy flopped into the saddle.

Freddy. "Kind of a tough crowd you run with, pig," he said. "Sounds like he comes from Texas. They breed some powerful wild mice out there." Then he turned and walked slowly up towards the woods. "Look at Cal," he said under his breath. "He's hoping I'll throw you and maybe break your neck, and then he'll have me and the fifty dollars both."

Freddy was too busy holding on to pay much attention to Mr. Flint. Cy's walk was only a gently swaying movement, but it was a long way to the ground and he held on tightly to the saddle horn. He couldn't reach the stirrups, but when they got into the woods the horse had him get down and showed him how to shorten the straps so that when he climbed back into the saddle his feet were supported. By the time they came down past the Big Woods into the Bean pastures Freddy had been taught how to steer by drawing the rein across the horse's neck, and how to hold himself in the saddle, and Cy had changed his gait to a sort of running walk which he called a singlefoot. "It's the easiest gait to ride," he said. "I'll teach you the others later." Even Quik began to enjoy himself, and untied his safety belt and climbed up to Freddy's shoulder.

During the next few days Freddy was in the saddle from early morning till long after dark. Like most fat people he had a good sense of balance so that he could sit easy and relaxed when the horse changed from a walk to a trot and from a trot to a canter, and Cy assured him that he had the makings of a fine horseman. Of course most of his friends were away on their search for adventure, and he was glad of that, for when they all came back in a week he would have something to surprise them with. To make the surprise a good one, he went down to the Busy Bee in Centerboro and bought a complete western outfit, as well as a saddle to take the place of the one lent by Mr. Flint.

It was when he was changing the things from the pockets of his coat to those of the handsome new red shirt that he came on the letter from the Horrible Ten. He had forgotten all about it in the excitement of buying a horse, but now the ten days they had given him was half gone. He looked at the knives drawn at the bottom of the page and shivered. If he could only write to these people and explain to them that there was some mistake, that he hadn't stolen any jewels, but he had no idea who or where they were.

So that afternoon after he had taken the saddle back to Mr. Flint he rode home through the woods and stopped by the big tree in which Old Whibley, the owl, lived, and rapped on the trunk. Quik, who had become very friendly with Cy, and enjoyed riding almost as much as Freddy did, had gone along, and now when there was no answer, Freddy asked him to run up and see if maybe the owl was asleep and hadn't heard his knock. So the mouse ran up the tree trunk and disappeared.

Almost at once there was a great scrabbling and squeaking up in the tree. Freddy could hear Quik's voice. "Oh, please! Please let me go! Freddy sent me up to see if you were here. I'm Quik, one of Mrs. Bean's mice. She'll be awful mad if you don't let me go."

There was a deep hooting laugh from the owl. "A house mouse, hey? Way out here in the woods? A likely story!"

"But I am, I tell you!" Quik squeaked. "I belong to Mrs. Bean."

"I know Mrs. Bean," said Whibley. "Most estimable woman. Any mouse of hers would have good manners. Wouldn't come sneaking into my home when he thought I was out."

"Hey, Whibley!" Freddy called. "That's right; he's our mouse. I sent him up to see if you were home."

There was silence for a minute, then the big owl, carrying the struggling Quik in his beak, floated down soundlessly and perched on a limb above Freddy's head. "Well, you found out," he said crossly. "Take him and go home." And he dropped the mouse on the brim of Freddy's new ten-gallon hat.

"You big bully!" Quik squeaked, and shook his clenched paws at the owl, then darted down and into Freddy's pocket.

"Wait a minute, Whibley," said the pig. "I'm in trouble; I've come to ask your advice. Don't you know me?" And he took the hat off and looked up.

"Certainly I know you!" said Old Whibley. "Wish I didn't. Each time I see you you look sillier than the last one. Well, I'll give you the advice. Go home and take off those monkey clothes before some farmer catches you and ties you up in his cornfield to scare away the crows."

"Oh, listen, will you?" Freddy pleaded, and

pulled the paper out of his pocket. "Look, did you ever hear of the Horrible Ten?"

"I suppose you're one of 'em," said the owl. "Well, you've proved it." He gave a hoot of laughter.

Freddy stared at him for a minute without saying anything. Then slowly he put his hat on, reined the horse around, and started back the way he had come.

But he had only ridden a few yards when the owl drifted past him and lit on a branch ahead. "Come, come," he said gruffly, "hurt your feelings, did I? Don't be so touchy. It's just your coming up here in a fireman's shirt and a hat as big as a washtub—" He stopped. "Well, well, never mind. What's your trouble?"

When Freddy had told him and shown him the letter, he said, "Horrible Ten, hey? They can't be so horrible or they wouldn't make such a fuss about it."

"That's what I've been telling him all along," put in Cy. "I bet if he was to meet 'em and give a good deep growl, they'd just faint right away."

"I guess I'm the one that would faint away before I gave the deep growl," said Freddy. "If I only knew who they were—"

Old Whibley had been holding the letter down on the branch and examining it. He raised his head and stared at the pig with his fierce yellow eyes. "You're a detective, ain't you?" he said. "Or used to be. Don't know why I should have to teach a detective his business. Here." He handed the letter back. "Take that piece of paper home and look at it."

"But I have," Freddy protested. "I've read it fifty times."

"I said look at it; didn't say read it. That piece of paper's got a lot to tell you besides what's written on it."

Freddy looked at it hopelessly. "Well, it's— it's just an ordinary sheet of paper. And the writing—well, it isn't even written; it's printed in capitals."

"Why?" the owl asked.

"Why what?"

"Why is it printed, stupid?" the owl snapped. "Why isn't it written?"

"Oh, I see what you mean," said Freddy. "Whoever sent it printed it so I wouldn't recognize his handwriting. Why, then it must be someone I know!"

"Take the paper home and look at it," Old

Whibley repeated. "I'm not going to do your work for you." And he flew back up into his nest and disappeared.

"Kind of a cranky old bird," said Cy.

"He isn't, really," Freddy said. "He grumbles a lot, but he's helped me out of some bad holes. And he's right: I guess I just got so scared of this Horrible Ten that I forgot about doing any detective work on the letter. But now I look at the paper—Quik, you take a look; isn't this a sheet off the pad Mrs. Bean writes letters on?"

"Looks like it," said the mouse.

"There's a corner missing where it was torn off the pad," said Freddy. "Maybe it's still on the pad. And if it is—"

"You mean Mrs. Bean is the Horrible Ten? Golly, maybe she and Mr. Bean are the head of a band of robbers, and—"

"Oh, sure!" said Freddy sarcastically. "Probably they're planning to murder you mice for your money. For that ten cents Eeny claims he can't pay back to the bank. Well, let's go home and find out." He reined Cy around and started down through the woods.

Mrs. Bean was sitting on the back porch

shelling peas. "My land, Freddy," she said as he jumped off the pony and came up the steps, "You certainly made me think you're the Lone Ranger, the way you career around on that horse. Only I hope you haven't got as many enemies as he has; in that red shirt you're an awful bright target for a gunman."

"I've got an enemy all right," said the pig, and handed her the letter.

After she had read it she went in the house and got the pad, and sure enough the missing corner of the sheet of paper was still attached to it. "And somebody's been using my pen," she said, "Because they left the ink bottle uncorked. So I know it's not Mr. Bean who's the Horrible Ten, because he would no more think of leaving the cork out of the ink bottle than he would of going to bed without his nightcap on. So that leaves me and the mice and Jinx as suspects, since we're the only ones that have been in the house today."

"Well," said Freddy, "None of the mice can handle a pen, and you would never have written anything as slangy as 'Get smart, fat boy.' That kind of narrows it down."

"And remember what Jinx said when he left

the meeting," put in Quik.

"I was just thinking of that," Freddy said. "He could give us excitement—leave it to him; wasn't that it? Well, I suspected him all the time. Yes, sir, I said to myself: That's just the sort of joke Jinx thinks up. Horrible Ten! Pooh, who'd be fooled by anything as silly as that?"

"Yeah," said Quik solemnly, "Who would? Whose teeth chattered up there in the woods so's't he could hardly talk?"

"Why, I was just scaring myself for fun," said Freddy. "You know, the way you do when you read a ghost story? I've got a lot of imagination, and I just got to thinking, *if* the Horrible Ten were real, and *if* they were after me with knives—And you know, Quik," he said interrupting himself, "I'm really kind of disappointed that they're just Jinx. Because—well, there's something in what Charles said about danger being the spice of life. Yes, sir, if—"

"Oh, baloney!" said Quik rudely. "You've got a lot of imagination all right if you can pretend you were just playing at being scared up there in the woods. Look; I was in your pocket, pig; I could hear your heart jump like a frog in a barrel every time a leaf rustled."

"Now, now, animals," said Mrs. Bean calmly. "There's nothing to be ashamed of in being scared. You're wrong, Quik, to blame Freddy for it. But you're wrong, too, Freddy, to pretend you weren't. Now shake hands nicely and make up."

The mouse and the pig looked at each other and they both winked. It was no use trying to explain to Mrs. Bean that their argument wasn't serious. They never could make her understand that Quik had just been riding Freddy, and that Freddy was defending himself half in fun. She was pretty apt to think that when the animals were kidding one another they really meant everything they said. So they shook hands solemnly, and Freddy rode off to the pig pen, and Quik went in to take a nap in the cigar box under the stove.

Chapter 4

When the animals set out in search of adventure, Jinx went west. Neither business nor pleasure ever took the Bean animals in that direction. To the north beyond the Big Woods was Zenas Witherspoon's farm, and beyond that Mr. Camphor's estate on the lake. To the south across the valley was the Macy farm, and down the road to the east lay Centerboro. So when Jinx turned right out of the gate and headed west up the road he was soon in strange country.

On stretches where he could see some distance ahead he walked in the middle of the road, but when he came to a bend he stepped off into the bushes and approached it cautiously. For you never knew what might be hidden by the turn and more than one careless cat has spent a week or two in the hospital by stepping around a corner too quickly. All small animals have to be careful about such things.

For a mile or so nothing happened. The sun was hot and Jinx began to get cross. "If I'm going to have adventures, why don't I *have* 'em?" he grumbled. "I'm not going to walk to California! I might better have stayed home under the porch and had a nice comfortable snooze."

Pretty soon a farm truck came up behind him, and as it went past, he waved to the driver. The man looked pretty startled for a minute but then he waved back. Jinx felt better after that. It wasn't exactly an adventure, but probably the man had never had a cat wave to him before, and Jinx could tell by the way he kept turning around and looking back that he was wondering if it had really happened.

A little farther on a fat squirrel was sitting on the stone wall, and Jinx made a dash for him. Rather to his surprise he caught him.

The squirrel was pretty upset. "You wouldn't have caught me if I hadn't got a sprained ankle," he said. "Do you intend to eat me?"

"I don't think so," said Jinx. "Squirrels disagree with me. It's the fur, I think. Tickles going down." He grinned at his captive.

"You interested in mice?" said the squirrel. "I could put you on to a splendid thing in the mouse line. There is a barn over here full of them. Only you have to look out for traps. That's how I sprained my ankle—got caught in one yesterday."

"I don't eat squirrels and I don't eat mice," said Jinx severely. "Some of my best friends are mice. I hope I've got *some* decent feeling."

"I hope so too," said the squirrel. "So how about letting me go?"

"O K," said the cat. "Only first tell me where this barn is. I might look into it. Lot of traps, you said? I don't believe in traps."

So he let the squirrel go and followed him

down a lane past an old farmhouse to a dilapidated barn which seemed to be half full of hay. The door was open, but the squirrel said: "Better go in the back way; not so many traps," and led him around to the side where a board had been pulled off just above the foundation.

Jinx crouched close to the ground and went in very very slowly, feeling the way with his whiskers, for it was dark in the barn. His whiskers touched something to the left, and as he crept to the right they brushed something on that side too. He crouched down to wait until his eyes got used to the darkness. And pretty soon they did, and he saw that he was in a dangerous spot. He was lying under a heavy wooden crate, one end of which was propped up with a small stick. It was this stick that his whiskers had touched, and if he had hit it, it would have slipped aside and the crate would have come down with a bang and trapped him.

"H'm," said Jinx to himself, "a box trap. Some boy trying to trap skunks, I suppose. That squirrel sent me in here on purpose. Now I wonder—" He peered cautiously out of the hole. The squirrel was sitting on a fence post, looking expectantly towards the barn. Jinx grinned to himself and then went back and with a swipe of his paw knocked out the stick. Down came the crate with a bang. Jinx let out a good loud screech, and then he called: "Help! Help!" There was no reply, but there was a rustling of small animals in the hay, and a little squeaky voice said: "Hold it, mister. If you want to catch Taffy, keep out of sight. He'll be in to make a deal with you in a few minutes."

"Who's Taffy?" Jinx asked.

"That squirrel that got you to come in here. I hope you give him a good licking, mister. He's given us a lot of trouble around here."

"Ain't you Beans' cat?" another voice asked. And when Jinx said he was, a mouse hopped out of the hay and came towards him. "Come on, boys," he said. "This guy is O K. Remember?—we went down and voted at an election they had on his farm a couple years ago."

"That's right," said Jinx. "That was when Mrs. Wiggins was elected President of the First Animal Republic. My, my, that seems a long time ago! So you boys came down and voted, eh? Well, come on out and tell me what this Taffy's racket is."

Five or six mice came rather timidly out of

the hay. One of them said: "The boy up at the house made this trap. He wanted to catch a skunk. Well, he caught two or three, but he never knew it, because Taffy let them out. He made them pay to get out, of course. I know one skunk's family that had to bring Taffy three hundred butternuts before he'd let their uncle go. He's one of the wealthiest squirrels in the county; they say he has twenty or thirty bushels of nuts hidden around different places."

"He does the same thing with us," said another mouse. "He's got some traps the boy had —those little cages that you go in and touch the bait and the door smacks shut on you. Of course the older mice don't get caught much, but some of the children, they always think they're smart enough to eat the cheese without springing the trap. There's one of my boys I've had to pay for five times. Keeps me poor, I tell you."

"There's ways I could show you of beating traps," said Jinx. "But this big box trap—no squirrel can lift this up to let anybody out."

"Ten squirrels can," said the mouse. "Taffy doesn't work alone; he's got a gang— Look out, here he comes, mister."

A shadow fell across the hole in the barn wall,

and the squirrel's voice said: "Hello! What's the matter in there?"

"I'm trapped," Jinx wailed. "Oh help me, good kind squirrel!"

"Oh my dear friend," said the squirrel in an oily voice, "how gladly would I rush to your assistance. But what can one poor squirrel do? But wait; it is just possible that if we had enough squirrels . . . though the squirrels in this neighborhood—I am sorry to have to say it, but they'll never help anybody unless they get paid for it. Of course if you had something you could pay them with—"

"I might be able to scrape together a little something," said Jinx. "I am not a cat of wealth. I have no vast possessions, no embroidered cushions, no herds of fat mice. (Excuse me, boys," he whispered to the mice. "My imagination sometimes runs away with me.) But possibly a few bags of acorns—"

"No acorns," said Taffy sharply. "We—that is, these squirrels I spoke of don't care for acorns. Black walnuts are in great demand. If you could manage say half a bushel of them—"

"Oh, yes," said Jinx eagerly. "I can do that.

Mr. Bean has two or three bushels stored in the attic."

Evidently Taffy's gang had been waiting outside with him, for now they all trooped in, a dozen or more of them. Their eyes were not yet used to the darkness, but under their leader's direction they lined up on one end of the crate and started to lift. Jinx was standing beside the crate. He could see Taffy peering through the slats, trying to see him. But the squirrel was not suspicious. A black cat in a dark barn is almost invisible.

Taffy didn't do any of the lifting, but stood back and bossed the job. "All right, boys; now *heave! ho! . . . heave! . . .* Come out, cat, when it's high enough. *Heave!*"

The squirrels had to get under the end of the crate to lift it high enough, and when they were well under, Jinx leaped. He leaped high and landed hard on the edge of the crate, which came down with a bang, knocking the squirrels every which way and pinning several under it. Then he leaped again and caught Taffy just as he was making a dash for the outside.

The squirrel didn't put up a fight. He just

lay quietly on his back with Jinx's paw on his chest. "Oh, come, come, my friend," he said reproachfully, "no violence, I beg! You were not in the trap at all, eh? Very clever of you. But of course you will understand this was all just a joke. Now just let me up, my dear fellow, and we'll go outside and talk it over. We'll have a good laugh over it together."

"Yeah?" said Jinx. "I'm having a good laugh right now." He had half expected that Taffy's friends would rally round and put up a fight to rescue their leader, but a glance over his shoulder assured him that those who were not caught under the crate had run away. It told him too that of the three who were pinned down none was badly hurt, though they were yelling and making a good deal of noise. "I suppose," he said, "that you swallowed all that stuff about my not eating squirrels. Well, that was *my* little joke. Ha, ha! Come on, Taffy, where's that good laugh we were going to have together?" And he held Taffy down with one paw and tickled him with the other until the squirrel shrieked with laughter.

"Well, well," he said after a time, "you're kind of overdoing it, aren't you? 'Tisn't as funny

The crate came down with a bang!

as all that." He called to the mice and asked them if they had any string, and when after a few minutes half a dozen of them came rolling along a ball of baling twine, he had them gnaw off a few lengths and then tied Taffy up. "Now," he said, "I want a piece of wood—a shingle would do—to drag him home on. I can't carry him. And I don't want to eat him here. Just had lunch an hour ago."

The mice found a shingle and gnawed a hole in it to put the twine through so that Jinx could pull it after him like a sled.

"What you really going to do with him, mister?" one of them asked.

Jinx winked at him. He hadn't as a matter of fact, any idea what to do with Taffy, except to get him far enough away from his traps so that he could never get back. He had thought that if he could get to the Beans', his friends could help maybe to take him to Centerboro and load him onto a freight car down by the railroad station. By the time he gnawed the cords off and got free, the train would be moving, and he might be out in Iowa or Kansas before it stopped and he could get off.

Cats aren't exactly lazy animals, but they

don't really enjoy hard work; and it was going to be good hard work to drag Taffy all the way back to the Beans' on that shingle. "You got any ideas?" he asked the mice.

The mice had plenty of ideas, most of them pretty ferocious.

But Jinx shook his head. "No," he said, "I don't blame you, boys, but this guy hasn't been guilty of murder or anything like that. He's just a cheap racketeer. I tell you what. You drag him down to the Bean farm for me. It's only four miles. I'll take care of him after that."

But mice don't like hard work any more than cats do. They said it would be easier to drag him down to the creek and throw him in. Jinx argued and the mice argued. Finally they struck a bargain. Jinx had remarked that he could teach them how to beat traps, and they said that if he would stay a day or two and give them and their children instruction in this difficult subject, they would haul Taffy down for him.

There were eighteen grown-up mice in the barn, and about as many children. They were all field mice. House mice are taught all about traps in the second grade, but field mice get no such instruction; indeed many field mice who live up in the hills get no schooling at all. So Jinx agreed, and as soon as he had released the three squirrels who were caught under the crate and boxed their ears and chased them away, he untied Taffy and shut him up in one of those mousetraps that are like little cages. And then he gathered the mice around him and gave them their first lesson.

Chapter 5

Jinx liked teaching so well that he stayed four days in the barn. There were several kinds of mousetraps around, and he showed the mice how they could spring some of them by poking at the bait with a twig, and then eat the bait in safety; and how those that were like cages could be entered safely if before you sprung them you put something large like a potato in the doorway, so the door wouldn't shut. He showed them how to escape from owls and hawks if they were caught in the open. Most mice, he said, tried to get away by running. But that was silly. The thing to do was to stand still; then, when the hawk made his pounce, dodge quickly to one side. The bird would get a clawful of grass, and while he was calling you names and flapping about, getting altitude for another dive, you had time to run ten or fifteen yards towards shelter. Then when he dove again, work the same trick.

"A bird can't change the direction of his pounce in the last half second," Jinx told them. "I know it's hard to stand still and watch those big claws coming down at you. But if you'll wait till that last half second, you'll always get away."

One of the mice suggested that they would also like to know how to escape from cats.

"I'm afraid I can't help you much there," Jinx said. "Cats—well, that's something else again. Being a cat myself, it ill becomes me to praise their cleverness and resourcefulness, but you have asked me, and I shall not conceal the truth from you. The cat is the most accomplished animal ever created. If he wants to catch you—well, you're just caught, that's all."

"I got away from a cat once," said a small mouse with large ears.

Jinx's whiskers twitched, but he said politely: "I congratulate you. I was just going on to say that while it is almost a complete waste of time to try to escape from a cat, there are a few dodges which I think I can teach you. Perhaps you, sir, will assist me. What is your name?"

The mouse said his name was Howard.

"Very well, Howard," said Jinx. "You stand over there against the wall. If you can reach either corner of the barn before I can catch you—well, you're pretty smart. Start whenever you like."

So Howard started. But he didn't run. He crept an inch or so, then he stopped, then he crept another inch.

"Don't be scared," said Jinx kindly, "I won't use my claws."

"I'm not scared," said Howard. And suddenly he turned and darted back the way he had come.

Jinx crouched, lashing his tail. "Now I'll show you," he said and leaped.

But instead of running away, Howard ran

straight for the cat. He dashed under him while he was in the air, and then while Jinx was wildly looking for him he ran over to the corner of the barn. "Did I do all right?" he asked eagerly.

Jinx had some trouble concealing his vexation. He began to wish he hadn't talked so big about cats. "Fine!" he said heartily. "Fine! Let's try it again."

Howard started the same way. He crept a little, stood still, then crept on. And Jinx crept too. He went forward fast and close to the ground. No mouse was going to run under him again. When he made his final pounce he was only three feet from Howard. But Howard wasn't there this time either. He ran straight up the wall, across on a beam, and dropped down into a corner.

Jinx sat down and looked around fiercely at the other mice, but none of them laughed. "Well, well," he said, trying to sound as if everything was going just as he had expected, "that's fine, Howard. You seem to know two of the simpler dodges, so I won't have to teach you those, and we can go on to the more complicated ones. But first I would like to give you a little talk on another subject."

The talk he gave was a very instructive one. It was about the proper use of mouseholes. "Let's say that you've got a cat watching a mousehole, and inside you've got a mouse trying to watch the cat. Pretty soon the mouse thinks: 'Guess he's gone' and he sticks his nose out. Bam! Down comes a big paw. The mouse jerks back and almost has heart failure. But after another hour of waiting he thinks: 'Surely he's gone now!' and out goes his nose again.

"Well, only one of these guys is going to lose in this kind of a game, and that's the mouse. And yet I never knew but one mouse who was smart enough to install some kind of a warning system. He lived in a house where there were four cats; but he never got caught because while he had only one doorway—a mousehole in the baseboard in the corner of the dining room—he had gnawed two or three peepholes on each side of the room, just big enough to look out of. The cats didn't even know they were there. He'd put one of his kids at each peephole, and when he'd heard 'em all say:

'O K, Pop,' he'd go out and clean up the crumbs on the dining room rug."

Well every day Jinx would lecture for an hour in the morning on some such subject as "Cats, and How to Escape Them," or "Safety Measures to Be Taken in Open Country," and then the afternoon would be devoted to field work, or supervised peephole-gnawing or personal camouflage in the barn.

Howard was Jinx's best pupil. The cat got very fond of him, and when at last on the fifth day Jinx said he would really have to be getting back home he asked the mouse if he wouldn't like to come and spend the rest of the summer on the Bean farm, and Howard was delighted.

So they tied lengths of cord to Taffy's cage and two mice took hold of each cord, and they dragged the cage out of the barn and down the lane and started along the road with it.

Of course Jinx realized that if a car came along, his little procession would cause a good deal of excitement. So he didn't take one of the cords. He followed along behind, dragging a leafy branch that had blown off in a windstorm a few days earlier, and when they heard a car coming he would pull the branch right over the cage and the mice, and then sit beside it until the car had passed.

They had almost reached the Bean farm when they heard a strange sound, one not often heard on eastern roads nowadays—the drumming rattle of the hoofs of a dozen horses coming along the hard macadam. Jinx pulled the branch over the cage just as the riders swept around the bend ahead at a fast trot.

The leader was a tall sour-faced man in cowboy clothes, and behind him, two by two, rode some of the gaudiest dressed people, Jinx thought, that he had ever seen outside a circus. The leader, of course, was Cal Flint, and the riders were the dudes who were boarding at his ranch, though Jinx didn't know that then. And the dudes wore western clothing of every color in the rainbow. Some of them rode easily, but most of them bounced and jiggled in their saddles until the cat thought they must have shaken all their teeth loose.

Mr. Flint held up one hand and the riders pulled up.

"What's wrong?" someone asked.

"Cats—I don't like 'em," said Mr. Flint as he swung out of the saddle and walked, with his big Mexican spurs clinking at every step, towards Jinx.

Jinx was not afraid of people. In general he had found them pretty well behaved. But there was something in Mr. Flint's expression that made him suspicious. The man didn't look as if he was coming over to scratch his head and say "Pretty Pussy!" And then as Mr. Flint swung his foot back for a kick he dodged. The big boot grazed his ear, and two seconds later he was halfway up a tree.

There was a murmur of disapproval from the dudes, and one woman—she was a Mrs. Balloway from Syracuse, and a very nice person too, though she sat in the saddle like a sack of damp sand—she said: "Oh, now, see here, Mr. Flint; that cat's doing no harm; what do you want to kick it for?"

But Mr. Flint's kick had dislodged the branch, and although the mice had run off and hidden in the grass, the trap with its prisoner was in plain sight.

Mr. Flint pointed to it. "That's why!" he said. "That's a cat for you!—trappin' innocent little squirrels and dragging them off in cages to be cooked and eaten! Why, just look at the

"Yip, yip, yipeee-e-e!" and down the slope came a small plump cowboy.

poor little fellow!" And he picked up the cage and held it out to them.

Taffy just looked at them mournfully with his big squirrel eyes and squeezed out fat tears which rolled slowly down over his fur. He certainly did look pathetic.

The ladies in the party said, "Poor little fellow!" and "Isn't he sweet!" and the men glared and shook their fists at Jinx. And Mr. Flint pulled a big gun from the holster at his hip and pointed it up at the cat.

But Mrs. Balloway reined her horse up close to him and put a hand on his arm. "Innocent little squirrel, eh?" she said. "Guess you don't know much about squirrels. They rob birds' nests and eat young birds, and do more damage than any cat can even think up. Let him go if you want to, but don't shoot that cat if you want *me* as a boarder at your ranch."

Mr. Flint shrugged his shoulders. "O K," he said, "but I'll let the squirrel go later, where he'll be safe!" And he tied the trap to his saddle horn. "Also," he said, "I'll just throw a little warning at that cat." He whipped up the gun and fired.

The bullet clipped a leaf within an inch of

Jinx's nose. "Golly," he thought, "he really meant to hit me!" He tried to get round behind the tree trunk, but it wasn't big enough. But then just as Mr. Flint started to raise the gun again there came a distant yell: "Yip, yip, yipeee-e-e!" and down the slope of the pasture to the north of the road came galloping a small plump cowboy on a buckskin pony.

He had on a bright red shirt with a design of yellow and blue lightning flashes on it, and he waved his hat as he came yelling down towards them; but when he got to the wall that separated the field from the road, he crammed his hat down over his ears and pulled his horse to a stop.

"Hiya, folks!" he said. "What's all the shootin'?"

Some of the dudes began to giggle and make remarks behind their hands, for while as a pig Freddy was nothing to laugh at, as a cowboy he really was sort of funny looking. But Mrs. Balloway spoke up and explained what had happened. "And I hope you can stop him from doing any more shooting at that cat," she said. "The cat was only acting according to his nature."

"And a very wicked nature, too," said Freddy, looking up and seeing Jinx for the first time. But he gave no sign of recognizing his friend. "As a matter of fact," he went on, "the sheriff's got a posse out scouring the hills for this cat. He's a pet cat belonging to Mrs. Bean. Been missing for most a week. So as a member of the posse I'll just take charge of him. Come down, kitty-kitty-kitty. Sweet little kitty! Come along. We'll put a pretty red ribbon around your neck and give you a nice fish head for supper."

Jinx didn't much like fish, and he certainly didn't want any old fish head, and if Mrs. Bean had tied a ribbon around his neck he would have been so ashamed that he would have stayed under the porch for a week. But he had of course recognized Freddy, and although he couldn't figure out what the pig was doing in cowboy clothes and riding a pony, he felt that the only safe thing was to go with him. For Mr. Flint still had his gun in his hand. So he slid down and dropped on Cy's back. "Any more of that 'pretty kitty' stuff," he muttered, "and I'll sink a couple of claws in that fat back of yours, pig."

Mr. Flint slowly pushed the gun back in its

holster. "O K," he said shortly. "Let's get going, folks."

The troop started on. As they passed Freddy they stared hard at him and several of them giggled and made remarks behind their hands. Only Mrs. Balloway smiled and nodded to him and saluted him with a gloved finger touching her hat brim.

"Well, there's one that's got some decent manners anyway," Freddy grumbled.

"Probably she's half-blind," said Jinx. "That get-up of yours would make a cat laugh. In fact, it does make this cat laugh." And he opened his mouth and gave a good yell to show that it did. Then suddenly he stopped. "Gee whiz!" he said. "I forgot about Howard!"

"I'm here, mister," said the mouse, sticking his nose out of a crevice in the wall. "The rest of 'em have gone back home, but you said I could come with you."

So Jinx told Freddy about Howard and Taffy and his adventure in the old barn.

"It's all right with me if he comes along," Freddy said. "But it's really up to our home mice. He'll have to live with them, I suppose. What do you say, Quik?" Quik, who had been riding in the pocket of Freddy's thunder-and-lightning shirt, leaned out with his elbows on the edge of the pocket and frowned down at Howard. "I suppose it'll be all right," he said. "If he doesn't eat us out of house and home. I never knew a field mouse yet who didn't eat like a pi—I mean, like a pinguin," he said hurriedly.

"What's a pinguin?" Jinx asked, and Howard said: "I think he means a penguin. They're very greedy creatures, though seldom seen in this neighborhood."

Quik grinned at him gratefully, but Freddy said: "Penguin nothing! He started to say 'pig' and then couldn't change it into anything that made sense. I ought to make him walk home. As for you, young Howard, you'd better go back to your barn."

"Aw, what did I do?" the mouse protested.

"It's all right for these fellows to kid me," said Freddy, "they're old friends. But I'm a stranger to you. It's bad manners to make fun of a stranger."

The mouse looked at him steadily for a minute, and then his ears drooped and he turned and walked slowly back along the road. Freddy frowned. Howard was putting on an act all right; no one could look so pathetic unless he was acting. But Freddy did a good deal of acting himself, and he could appreciate it when somebody did a good job. "Oh, come on," he said with a grin, "you can go with us."

Chapter 6

Freddy had a couple of those folding garden
chairs with a long strip of canvas for back and
seat, that you can lie back and go to sleep in.
He had bought them at an auction, and they
were so rickety that if anyone weighing over
five pounds sat in them they just collapsed; but
when he had them out, one on each side of his
front door, he felt that they made the pig pen
look quite like a gentleman's country estate.
He was sitting that evening in the straight
chair in which he had presided over the com-

mittee meeting five days ago. Jinx was in one of the folding chairs and Quik and Howard in the other. Cy was wandering about making scrunching noises as he pulled up bites of grass with his teeth.

"I can't help thinking about that Taffy," Jinx said. "If Mr. Flint lets him go, he'll just go back and start that racket of his all over again."

"Don't you worry about that, cat," said Cy. "If old Flint was going to let him go, he'd have opened the trap right there."

"What do you mean, Cy?" Freddy asked, and the pony said, "Squirrel pot pie, that's what I mean. I know Flint. Even if he didn't like squirrel he'd eat him just to be ornery."

They all looked at him for a minute. Then Freddy said: "Why, that's pretty awful, specially after he promised to let him go. If I'd known that, I wouldn't have let him take the cage with him."

"Oh, yeah?" said Jinx. "You and who else?"

"Why him and me, cat," Cy said. "What do you say, Freddy, shall we go up to the ranch now and bring the squirrel back?"

But Freddy shook his head. "Jinx is right,

Cy," he said. "I guess I couldn't have done anything—especially as Flint had a gun."

"Well, you've got a gun there in your holster," said Jinx.

"It's just for show." Freddy drew it out. "A water pistol. But hey, wait a minute!" he said, jumping up. "I have too got a gun. You remember, Jinx, the one that we took away from that magician, Signor Zingo, remember?" He ran in and came out in a minute with a big pistol which he pushed into the holster, then tried pulling out two or three times.

"You aren't very quick on the draw, pardner," said Cy. "S'pose you could hit anything with it?"

Freddy backed off about ten feet from the pig pen, aimed at a knothole in the side wall, and pulled the trigger. There was a terrific bang, and a small round hole appeared about three feet to the left of the knothole.

The mice giggled and Jinx gave a sarcastic laugh. "Two-Gun Freddy, the Terror of the Plains!" he said. "Boy, I sure would hate to get in a shooting mix-up with you, specially if you were on my side."

Cy just shook his head. "You ain't supposed

to shut your eyes," he said. "Try it again and keep 'em open."

"Oh-oh!" said Jinx warningly. "Here comes trouble!" For Mr. Bean had come out of the back door and was walking up towards them.

Jinx and Freddy stood their ground, but the mice quietly ran off. Mr. Bean came up, holding out his hand for the gun. "Don't allow my animals to have firearms," he said. He hefted the pistol in his hand, looking from it to the knothole. "That your mark?" And when Freddy said it was, he raised the gun and fired. The bullet hit about two feet to the right of the knothole.

Mr. Bean shook his head. "Gun's no good," he said. "Shoots high and to the right."

Jinx winked at Freddy. If that was really so, then both bulletholes should have been to the right. But Freddy's was to the left.

"Say, Freddy," said Jinx, "what's back of that knothole—inside your house, I mean?"

"Oh, my land!" said the pig and dashed inside. Mr. Bean followed him. Perched on the typewriter where he had tossed it, was Freddy's ten gallon hat with a hole drilled neatly right through the crown. The other bullet had smacked into a framed enlargement of a snapshot of Mr. and Mrs. Bean, taken on their honeymoon, smashing the glass and replacing Mr. Bean's pictured head with a round black hole.

Mr. Bean made a sound which might have been hiccups or might have been chuckles—you couldn't tell behind all those whiskers. "Ain't such bad shots after all," he said. "Plugged each other. Guess I ought to thank you—you certainly improved my looks." He put a finger in the hole in the hat. "I'll get you a new hat. But I guess it ain't safe for either you or me to go round with a loaded gun in our pocket." He looked thoughtfully at the pig. "I suppose you want it to go with your cowboy suit, hey? Tell you what I'll do. I'll let you keep it if you promise to shoot nothing but blanks."

Freddy agreed readily enough. The damage they had done scared him. Suppose a bullet had smashed his typewriter? Or even gone right through the pig pen and hit one of his friends?

They came outside and Mr. Bean stood for a minute looking down towards the house. "Nice view," he said. Freddy thought it was, too, although as a matter of fact all anybody could see was the barnyard with the buildings grouped round it. I guess no stranger would have thought it specially beautiful or picturesque. But of course it was their own home, and that made a difference.

"Yes, sir; nice view," said Mr. Bean again, and before Freddy could stop him, he dropped down into the canvas chair where the mice had been sitting, and immediately smashed it and went down with a yell and a crash onto the ground.

Mrs. Bean came rushing to the back door. "Mr. B?" she called. "Oh, my land, wait a minute, I'll be right up. You want I should call the doctor?"

"Great grief!" Mr. Bean called back, as he got slowly to his feet. "Can't I sit down to rest for half a minute without you thinking I've collapsed?"

"What else do you want me to think?" she said. "I hear shooting, and then I see you lying on the ground. I never saw anyone sit down to rest that way before."

Mr. Bean just waved his hands at her and she turned and went into the house, and he said to Freddy: "Guess I'll go down before I bust anything else. I'll get you a new chair tomorrow."

When he had gone the mice came back, and after talking it over it was decided that if they were going to try to rescue Taffy, they ought to do it before he was made up into a pot pie. Whatever was done they would have to do by themselves, for the other farm animals were not due back from their adventuring for another day or so. So they decided to go up to the ranch that evening.

Freddy hadn't said anything when he came out about the damage the pistol bullets had done. He knew he'd never hear the last of it if Jinx knew about it. But he had not forgotten the letter from the Horrible Ten with which the cat had tried to scare him, and by and by he said, "Oh say, Jinx, I guess I didn't show you this," and brought it out.

"Golly!" said the cat. "Boy, you *are* in a spot if the Horrible Ten are after you! I've heard about those babies, and are they tough!"

Freddy shot a warning look at Quik, who seemed inclined to giggle. The mouse knew, of course, that Jinx was the one who had made up the Horrible Ten in the first place. "That's right," Freddy said. "But I had a talk with one of 'em and I fixed it up."

"You had a wh-what?" Jinx demanded. He looked pretty startled.

"Seems they were after the wrong party," Freddy went on. "They said they were sorry they scared me, and promised they wouldn't bother me any more." He frowned gloomily. "But I sure would hate to be that other party."

"Yeah," said Jinx slowly. "Yeah. But this—well, now, this one you talked to: Who was he? What did he look like?"

"They don't have names," Freddy said. "They're just Horrible One, Horrible Two, and so on. He was Horrible Five. Little, and sort of black all over, with long pointed teeth. Blue teeth. And a knife. A little sharp knife, sort of like an ice pick. He was really an awful looking thing—made me shiver. —Oh well, we don't have to worry about them."

Jinx eyed his friend suspiciously. He started to say something two or three times, then stopped. At last he gave sort of a hollow laugh and said: "Shucks, Freddy—the Horrible Ten! That's just strictly to laugh at. No gang ever had such a name. Somebody wrote that letter to you for a joke."

"That's what I thought at first," said the pig. "Until I saw one of 'em. Boy, they're nothing to laugh at. I'm glad it's not me they're after."

Jinx didn't say anything more but he was pretty thoughtful the rest of the day.

Along about supper time, when Jinx had gone to the house to get his milk, Freddy went down to the stable, and up in the loft where Uncle Ben had had his workshop he found a big sheet of shiny tin. With heavy shears he cut out ten narrow, pointed pieces four or five inches long and then hunted up Rabbit No. 23, who sometimes worked for him in the detective business, and gave him certain instructions.

Shortly before dark Freddy saddled Cy, and with Quik and Howard in his pockets and Jinx riding double behind him, started for Mr. Flint's ranch. They went up through the pasture, and across the back road, and cut through a corner of the Big Woods. It was still light out in the fields, but in the woods it was already dark, and you couldn't see things clearly. They came to a place where a fallen tree trunk blocked the way, and Cy had turned aside to go

"We are the Horrible Ten—"

around it when Freddy nudged him, and he stopped. His ears pricked up and turned forward towards the log. "Something queer going on here," he said.

"Well, that *is* queer," said Freddy, and both the mice said: "Gosh, yes!"

"Boloney!" said Jinx impatiently. "What's queer—you all scared of the dark?" And he laughed contemptuously.

But he only laughed for about a second, for up on the log jumped ten little creatures and each one held in his right forepaw a glittering knife. They capered up and down in a sort of dance and recited a verse in shrill little voices:

> *"We are the Horrible Ten,*
> *Neither animals nor men;*
> *Neither men nor animiles,*
> *And we're meaner than crocodiles,*
> *Much wickeder and horrider*
> *Than alligators in Florida.*
> *And we take our enemies' lives*
> *With our ten sharp little knives,*
> *In using which, our system*
> *Is to stick 'em in and twist 'em."*

If Jinx hadn't been so disturbed by what Freddy had told him about talking to one of the Horrible Ten, it might have occurred to him that the voices sounded very much like rabbits' voices, although the creatures had queer round heads which certainly didn't have rabbits' ears.

But he had written the Horrible Ten note as a sort of joke, and to prove that he could make life interesting for the pig, and he simply couldn't figure out how these little horrors he had made up could have talked to Freddy, or how they could appear like this. That is the way with practical jokers: they never can understand it when someone turns the joke around and plays it on them.

And the Horrible Ten went on:

"Our teeth are blue and our eyes are red;
We've got bad manners; we're not well bred.
We think it silly to be polite,
So we snatch and snarl and scratch and bite."

"Excuse me for interrupting," said Freddy. "But you—I mean, you don't think that we're your enemies, do you?"

They stopped prancing up and down, and

one of them said: "All animals are our enemies. But there's one special enemy we're after now —a cat named Jinx. You seen him around? What's that animal back of you on the saddle?"

"What's he done?" Freddy asked.

"He wrote a letter and signed our name to it," said the creature. "That's forgery, pig. Forgery and blackmail and impersonating a Horrible. Say, isn't that him back of you?"

"Sure it's him!" said another of them. He waved his knife. "Come on, Horribles, let's get him!" And they jumped down from the log and began creeping slowly towards the pony.

This was too much for Jinx. He was a little suspicious that somebody was putting up a game on him, but not sure enough of it to wait and take a chance with those gleaming little knives. He gave a yell and jumped down and streaked for home.

"Thanks, boys," said Freddy. "Quit laughing, will you, Cy? You'll shake me out of the saddle."

"Look, Freddy," said the head Horrible, "can we keep these imitation knives?" He came closer and I don't suppose you would have recognized him as a rabbit even then, for he had his ears tied down. That was one reason why Jinx hadn't known him. "We'd like to work this gag on Charles. He's been awful snooty to us rabbits lately."

"Well," said Freddy slowly, "I guess it's all right. Only go kind of easy. It never does to carry a joke too far. Somebody might get hurt."

So the rabbit thanked him, and then as he and Cy started on up through the woods, the ten Horribles started back towards the Bean farm, marching two by two, and singing as they went:

> *"Oh, horrible indeed are we;*
> *To look at we are awful!*
> *We shout and howl and yell with glee*
> *When doing deeds unlawful.*
> *So let our enemies beware,*
> *And hide in caves and cellars,*
> *For when we catch one by the hair,*
> *We pinch him till he bellers.*

> *"Oh, we are the Ten, the Horrible Ten,*
> *Bears, when they hear us, cower in their den,*
> *Elephants tremble, and lions shudder—*
> *Hide their heads and yell for their mudder."*

The sound died away. "Those dopes are going to get into trouble," said Quik.

"They can run pretty fast," said Freddy. "We've got troubles of our own to worry about. There are the ranch house lights through the trees."

Chapter 7

At the edge of the open fields Freddy dismounted and unsaddled Cy, and the pony trotted on down towards the house. It was getting so dark now that there wasn't much chance of his being noticed, and if he was, nobody would be surprised to see another horse wandering around. As it happened, he made the rescue easily; the trap with the squirrel inside it had been hung up in the cookhouse, and Cy just lifted it down and brought it back to Freddy in his teeth.

"This guy wants to make a deal with you," Cy said. "Tell him, squirrel."

So Taffy stuck his nose against the wires of the cage and rolled his eyes mournfully at Freddy, and said: "Oh, Mr. Pig—good kind Mr. Pig, I shall always be grateful to you for saving me from being a pot pie, and my heart is full of gratitude—"

Freddy interrupted him. "Don't call me Mr. Pig! My name is Freddy. And you can save your gratitude because *my* heart is full of disgust. We rescued you because we didn't want you made into a rather inferior stew, but you're staying in that cage until we can ship you out of the state."

"Oh," said the squirrel. And then he shrugged his shoulders and said: "Very well, my friend; very well. I was going to give you some important information in exchange for my freedom. But of course if the safety of your bank means nothing to you—"

"If you're talking about the First Animal Bank," Freddy said, "bandits have made several attempts to rob it in the past. They didn't succeed. I'm not worried about anything Mr. Flint could do."

Taffy looked at him in amazement. "How did you know about that?" he demanded.

Of course Freddy didn't know about any plan of Mr. Flint's. But he remembered how suspicious he had been of the man's interest in the bank, and he guessed that Taffy had heard something at the ranch about it.

"My goodness," he said, "what kind of a detective do you think I'd be if I didn't know about such things?"

Quik had climbed up to Freddy's shoulder. "Hey, quit bluffing, will you, pig?" he whispered. "Find out what the guy knows. Remember I have fourteen cents as well as a sack of cheese rinds in your darned old bank."

Freddy said to Taffy: "I know pretty well what they're up to. There are one or two details, however, that I have not yet learned. So that if you want to tell me what you know I might—mind you, I'm only saying that I *might* —let you go free. Under certain conditions, of course."

Taffy asked what details he wanted to know.

"I want to know when Flint plans to rob the

bank, and I want to know who is in it with him."

"You call those 'details'?" Taffy demanded. "I call it the whole story. And if you want it, you'll have to pay for it by turning me loose."

"I don't want it that bad," said Freddy.

He swung up into the saddle and turned Cy's head homeward, and although Quik kept trying to get his attention, he said nothing more until when they were nearly home, they caught up with the Horrible Ten, who were marching along, two by two and still singing.

"Hey, Horribles!" Freddy called, and they broke ranks and crowded up around the pony. "I've got a prisoner here," he said, "and he's got some information he doesn't seem to want to give me. Suppose you could tickle him up with your knives and persuade him to talk?"

He winked at Rabbit No. 23, who was the head Horrible, and No. 23 winked back, and then turned to his followers. "Brother Horribles," he said, "are your knives sharp?"

"Sharp as razors, Your Dreadfulness," said the rabbits.

"Are they thirsty?"

"They thirst for squirrel's blood, Your Dread-fulness."

"Release the prisoner, pig," said No. 23 solemnly.

"Just a minute!" Taffy's voice rose to a desperate squeak. "Look, pig; I'll talk—I'll tell you! Don't let these—these things grab me!" He shivered as he looked down at the Horribles, who were war-dancing in a circle, waving their knives.

So Freddy nodded to No. 23, and the rabbits drew off a little way, and then Taffy told them what he knew. It wasn't a great deal. He had overheard Mr. Flint and two of the cowboys who worked for him, Slim and Jasper, planning to break into the bank. They were going to ride down, cut the alarm bell rope, and then go down into the vaults and steal anything valuable they could find. "That pig is suspicious right now," Mr. Flint had said. "So we'll wait a week or so. It's a cinch. Place is run by a bunch of animals; what could they do even if they caught us there? And suppose they recognize us—who's going to take the word of a pig on the witness stand?"

"And now, Mr. Pig, won't you please let me go?" Taffy begged.

Freddy looked at him thoughtfully, then he put the cage down on the ground and held a whispered consultation with No. 23.

"Brother Horribles," said No. 23, "gather round and look upon the prisoner."

The rabbits crowded up and peered through the wires, and some of them poked at the cowering Taffy with their knives.

"Brother Horribles," said No. 23, "you will recognize the prisoner again?"

"Yes, Your Dreadfulness."

"And if the order is given, you will find him, wherever he is, and chop him into very small pieces?"

"With pleasure, Your Dreadfulness."

"Good. We will now withdraw, Brother Horribles."

So the rabbits marched off, and when they had gone Freddy opened the cage. "You can go home," he said to Taffy. "And you'll be perfectly safe as long as you behave yourself. But if I hear of your holding any more animals for ransom—well, I guess you know who'll come calling on you some night."

So Taffy slunk off, and Freddy went on home. It wasn't until next morning when he was saddling Cy to ride in to Centerboro to buy blank cartridges for his gun, that he saw Jinx. The cat came strolling up from the barnyard, stopping here to sniff at a daisy, there to tap playfully at a scurrying ant; putting on an elaborate show of having nothing on his mind, nothing at all. Freddy grinned: he knew what was bothering his friend.

"Morning, Jinx," he said. "Still all in one piece, I'm happy to see. The Horrible Ten didn't get you, then?"

Jinx sniffed contemptuously. "Who, them? They'd better not try it!"

"They were around asking about you earlier this morning," said the pig.

Jinx sniffed again. "Oh, yeah?" He watched Freddy tighten the cinch and swing himself into the saddle, then he said suddenly, "Hey, wait a minute. Look, Freddy; this Horrible outfit—well, there aren't any such animals, are there?"

"My goodness," said the pig, "you saw 'em, same as I did. Of course when I got that letter I thought it was just a joke. To tell you the truth, I thought maybe you were the one that sent it to me. But then—golly, there the things were, knives and all! Awful, weren't they?"

"Well, I suppose I'd better tell you," said the cat. "I did write the letter. I made up the Horrible Ten. Shucks, it was just a joke! But it isn't a joke any more. How could they come alive, Freddy, when I just *thought* 'em?"

"Oh, well," said Freddy, "as long as you've owned up to it, I ought to tell you who they are." And he did.

There was one good thing about Jinx, he could laugh just as hard when the joke was on himself as when it was on someone else. He just lay down and rolled in the grass. "Rabbits!" he said. "Me lying awake all last night for fear rabbits were after me! You wait till I get hold of that 23."

"You mustn't do anything to him, Jinx," Freddy said. "I was the one that put him up to it."

"Shucks, I want to congratulate him. Guess I'll go up now and see if he's home." And he trotted off.

When Freddy set out to do something, he

was never satisfied with just halfway doing it. To have a horse and a cowboy suit and a gun belt with two guns in it would have been enough for some people. But not for him. He was determined to learn how to ride and shoot and handle a rope as well as any real cowboy. And because he wanted to learn, he learned quickly. He had a good teacher in Cy, and within a few days he could stick tight to the saddle while the pony whirled and crow-hopped and bucked and reared. Of course Cy didn't really try to throw Freddy. He could have done that easily. But he tried to give the pig as much as he could take, and Freddy could take a little more every day.

Freddy was getting quick on the draw, too. He had practised by the hour, and now when Cy gave the signal he could yank both guns— the real one and the water pistol—out of their holsters and point them and pull the triggers, all inside of a single second.

Freddy didn't neglect other sides of life on the range either. There was an old guitar in the Bean attic. Before they were married, Mr. Bean used to serenade Mrs. Bean with it. Some unkind people said that she married him in order to stop the racket, but this doesn't make sense, for when he sang, Mr. Bean's voice was just a sort of grumble—so low that you could hardly hear it. Freddy got the guitar out and strung and tuned it, and he worked away at it evenings until he could strum a pretty good accompaniment to *Home on the Range* and other such songs.

In the evening, two days after Taffy's rescue, Freddy was sitting out in the new canvas chair Mr. Bean had bought him, twanging his guitar in the moonlight, when Charles came down through the pasture.

"Hi, rooster," said Freddy. "Back from your travels? Did you have any adventures?"

"Adventures!" said Charles bitterly. "I knew how it would be when Henrietta insisted on coming along. You can't take your wife along when you ride out in search of adventure. Because what happens? Instead of looking for adventure you go visit all her relatives. And she's got relatives in every chicken coop in the county. Just as sure as I saw a nice likely looking piece of road or a patch of woods where some real adventure might be waiting, Henri-

He worked until he could strum a good accompaniment.

etta would say: 'Come along, Charles; Cousin Eunice lives down this lane,' and we'd drop in and stay a couple days.

"Well, late this afternoon we were up by the end of the lake, and we saw a lot of cowboys sitting around a campfire, and I wanted to go over and see what was going on. But no, Aunt Effie Peck lived up the road a piece, and we had to go see her. She's another of 'em. She's just like a radio, except she don't even pause for station identification. So I quit. I sneaked off home. I been talked to death by relatives, Freddy. And now I'm going down to the henhouse and get some sleep before Henrietta gets back. Adventures—ha!" And he started wearily on.

He hadn't gone more than a dozen yards when ten little round heads popped up out of the grass in front of him, and ten little glittering knives were waved menacingly at him. They sang their song and began to do their war dance, working around behind Charles so that the startled rooster was surrounded.

"Hey!" he squawked. "What is this? Get out of here—let me alone!"

They stopped their dance, and the head Horrible said: "Brother Horribles, what would you like for supper?"

"We would like rooster hash, Your Dreadfulness," they replied.

"And how would you go about preparing this delicious dish, Brother Horribles?"

"First we would grab this rooster and chop him up small with our little knives, Your Dreadfulness, and then—"

Neither Charles, cowering in the bloodthirsty circle, nor the Horrible Ten had noticed Henrietta coming down the hill. She paused for a moment, and then with an angry squawk and a flutter of wings she plunged down into them, scattering the rabbits, who squeaked in terror as her sharp beak nipped them. In half a minute every Horrible had vanished.

Henrietta then pounced angrily on Charles. "You!" she said. "A fine one you'd be to go wandering off by yourself in search of adventure! If I leave you alone five minutes you're in trouble. Get along home with you!" And she chased him off down to the henhouse.

Chapter 8

The animals who had set out in search of adventure began wandering back home next day, and at a meeting in the barn that night they told their stories. With the exception of Charles they had all had a good time, and some of the stories were quite exciting. Mrs. Wiggins, who had had the foresight to take some money with her, had stopped at an antique shop along the road and bought a hand-painted fire shovel for

Mrs. Bean—it had a little winter scene on the shovel part and roses on the handle, and she got a moustache cup for Mr. Bean.

These are the cups that have a little flat sort of a china guard built into them just inside the rim, which is supposed to press against your moustache—if you have one—and keep it from getting into the coffee. Mr. Bean was very much pleased with the cup, although in spite of having such bushy whiskers he was a very neat drinker and seldom got his moustache even damp.

The woman who kept the antique shop had tried to push Mrs. Wiggins out when she first went in, but when she saw that the cow had money she let her look around, although some other customers left rather hurriedly. But later they sat on the porch and talked and got quite friendly, and Mrs. Wiggins stayed on for a week and tended the shop every day when the owner went to visit her sick aunt in the hospital.

When Freddy told his story and they heard that there was danger that Mr. Flint might try to rob the bank, the animals began to look worried. Many of the smaller animals—the squirrels and rabbits and mice—had their entire next winter's supply of food in the vaults, and nearly all the animals on the farm had brought money to the bank for safekeeping. It may surprise many people to learn that animals have money since they never work for wages, and have no pockets to carry money in if they did. But animals, when they are walking along, keep their eyes on the ground more than people do, and it is surprising how many coins they find. Even the woods animals often find money and valuables that hunters and hikers have dropped. I know one fox who has a large cameo brooch set with diamonds, and there is a black snake down on the flats who owns two wrist watches which he wears when he goes to parties. Alice and Emma, the two ducks, have some very handsome jewelry which they found when rummaging around for food in the mud at the bottom of their pond. And a lot of money rolls behind baseboards and is found by mice. Many mice have piggy banks.

Naturally the animals were worried, and they demanded to know what precautions Freddy had taken to safeguard their property.

"I've put on extra guards at the bank," he said, "and I'm keeping an eye on things. Don't you worry; your stuff is safe."

"That's what *you* say," said Bill, the goat. "I've got a dozen pairs of fine old well-aged boots down in your bank vaults. I've been saving them for when my folks come to visit, so we can have a real high-class banquet. It took me two years to get that lot together, and I'm not going to lose them now just because you want to spend your time galloping around in a monkey suit yelling 'Yippee!' instead of tending to your business."

There was a murmur of agreement from the other animals, and Mrs. Wiggins said, "You can't blame Bill, Freddy. All of us have got valuables in the bank, and you're responsible for them. That Flint is no better than a bandit, and until he's out of this country, nothing will be safe."

"All right, all right," said Freddy irritably. "I'll do something—I promise I'll do something about him."

"Yeah?" said Bill. "When?"

Freddy of course had no idea what he could do, much less when he could do it. But he knew that he had to act as if he was doing something. Otherwise the animals would take all their

valuables back into their own keeping, and the
First Animal Bank would have to close its doors
and go out of business. So he put a look of great
determination on his face, got up, jammed his
ten-gallon hat down over his ears and buckled
on his gun belt, which he had laid aside during
the meeting; and then he said: "Come on Cy,
we'll settle this," and followed by the pony,
went out into the night. It came near being one
of the worst mistakes of his entire career.

Freddy stopped at the pig pen to saddle Cy,
then rode up through the pasture towards the
woods. Cy said, "You can't shoot Flint with
nothing but blanks in your gun."

"Who said I was going to shoot Flint?"
Freddy asked.

"That's where your friends think you're going," said the pony. "The way you said you'd
settle things. They think you're going up to
challenge him to a pistol fight. And if I'm not
mistaken—" He stopped and looked back. "Yes,
they're coming after you. They're coming to
back you up, Freddy."

The moon was just rising, and by its light
Freddy could see several figures moving across
the barnyard; yes, they were following. "Oh,

my goodness!" he said. "What'll we do, Cy? When I said we'd settle things, I didn't mean I was going to fight Mr. Flint; I just meant—well, I don't know what I did mean. I guess I was just putting up a bluff. I figured maybe I'd think of something before we got to the ranch."

"In that case," the pony said, "the best thing to do is go back and tell them it was just a bluff. Or no, you can't do that—that'll ruin you. Tell 'em—lemme see—tell 'em you've been thinking it over and you don't think it would be right to shoot Mr. Flint, because after all, he hasn't really robbed the bank yet."

"I wish I'd never got into this cowboy business," said Freddy. "If you're going to be a cowboy, you can't back down once you've started something like that. If I've let 'em think I'm going to fight Flint, I'll have to go through with it. Is Flint a good shot?"

Cy said: "Flint's sure of himself with a gun, because now he knows you can't shoot. He's a coward, though in some ways. He hates hatchets and knives—anything that cuts. If you was to go after him with a knife he'd get right down on his knees and beg for mercy. Funny thing different folks are afraid of. Now me, I'm

deathly afraid of barns at night. The inside of
'em, I mean. All black and there's noises—
things scurryin' around. Wow! It gives me
the—"

"Sure, sure," said Freddy; "very ghastly. But
how good a shot is he?"

"Look, Freddy," said Cy, "even if you
mounted a machine gun on your saddle you
wouldn't have a chance with him. He has a
regular stunt he does: sets up tin cans on the
posts of the corral fence, and then rides past
'em at a gallop and he'll plug three or four
right off the posts."

"I'm a lot bigger than a tin can," said Freddy.

"Maybe he wouldn't hit a vital spot," Cy
suggested.

By this time Freddy's friends had nearly
caught up with him. "Hey, Freddy," Jinx
called; "come on give it up and come back.
We'll think of something better than you going
up there and getting yourself shot full of holes."

"Good land, Freddy," said Mrs. Wiggins,
"we didn't mean for you to get into a fight."

Freddy had no intention of getting into a
fight if he could help it, but he had a reputation
to keep up. That is the trouble with a reputa-

tion. You go and build up a reputation for bravery, and then the first thing you know, there's a fight on your hands. And maybe you don't feel specially brave that morning. But you've got to act as if you did. So Freddy sat up very straight in the saddle and slapped his pistol holster and looked noble—it is easy to look noble by moonlight—and he said: "My friends, do not attempt to turn me from my purpose. You have appealed to me, and I intend to do my duty."

For a minute none of the animals, who had now all come up, said anything, and Freddy was sorry that he had spoken with such determination. "They might at least put up an argument," he thought. "But no; what do they care? Just an old friend going out to be blown to smithereens, that's all."

Then Hank said hesitatingly: "Well, I dunno; seems as if—" He stopped.

"Yes?" said Freddy eagerly.

"Oh, nothing," said Hank. "Nothing."

Freddy got mad. "Oh, go on back to the farm, will you," he said.

"Why, we came up to help you," said Mrs. Wiggins. "If there's a fight—"

"If there's a fight, I'll handle it," said Freddy. "Go on back; I know what I'm doing."

They shook their heads doubtfully, but they turned and started back. As soon as they were out of sight, Freddy dismounted and said: "Look, Cy, I'm beginning to get hold of the tail end of an idea. Suppose you could circle around down to the house without being seen and get the mice? They'll all be home from the meeting by this time. Tell 'em we're on a secret mission. And let's see—I'll meet you at the pig pen; I want to get some gum, and some string, and my guitar."

An hour later up by the ranch house the dudes were sitting around the campfire, listening to Mr. Flint who was telling stories of his experiences with cattle rustlers and outlaws. Mr. Flint was a good storyteller in spite of his creaky voice, and his stories were good stories, for he had got them all out of a book called *Bad Men of the Old West.* "Well sir," he drawled, "when I see them three hombres a-sneakin' up the draw, I knowed old Two-Quart Robinson had squealed. So I throwed down on 'em, and—" He stopped, for the twan-

gle of a guitar came out of the night and a
light but pleasing tenor voice sang:

"When the moon rides high on the pine tree
branch,
Then Two-Gun Freddy of the Lone Pig Ranch
(Oh, hi, yi, yippy-yippy-yip!)
He takes his guitar, and he tightens up the
strings,
And he jumps in the saddle, and this is what
he sings:

Oh, hi, yi, yippy-yippy-yings!
Oh, hi, yi, yippy-yippy-yap, yop, yowp,
Oh, hi, yi, yippy-yippy-yings!

"Oh, the wild wind moans o'er the lone prai-ree
But Two-Gun Freddy, oh, louder moans he;
(Sing hi, yi, yippy-yippy-yip!)
He shouts this song till the whole sky rings,
As he sits in the saddle and twangles on the
strings:
Oh, hi, yi, yippy-yippy-yings!
Oh, hi, yi, yippy-yippy-yap, yop, yowp,
Oh, hi, yi, yippy-yippy-yings!"

And then into the light of the campfire came walking a buckskin pony and on his back sat a small plump rider who sang and strummed a guitar.

The dudes applauded the song heartily, and Mr. Flint said: "Light down, stranger, and set." Then he peered across the fire at Freddy. "Seen you before somewheres."

"You shore have," said Freddy, trying to talk as western as possible. "Likely you've forgotten I bought this bronc off you the other day so's you wouldn't beat him to death."

Mr. Flint started up. "Now I know you," he said. "Sure, you bought the horse. But I'd go kind of easy on that talk about my beatin' him."

"Would you?" Freddy asked. "Well, you *were* beating him, you big bully."

Mr. Flint started to walk around the fire to come closer to Freddy, and then he remembered that Cy would probably take a piece out of his arm if he did and he stopped. "Out where I come from," he said, "that's fighting talk, pardner," and his right hand slipped down towards his pistol butt.

"We're not out where you come from," said Freddy. "And even if we were, I wouldn't fight

"Beat it," he said.

anybody like you." He felt pretty sure that Mr. Flint wouldn't do any shooting, particularly in front of all the dudes who were guests on his ranch.

"That's right smart of you, mister," said Mr. Flint sarcastically. "No sense gettin' your ears blown off." He pulled out his gun suddenly. "Beat it," he said.

Freddy gave a sudden squeal and wriggled in the saddle. "Quit that!" he said. He wasn't speaking to Mr. Flint. He had two mice in each of his shirt pockets. Quik and Howard were in one, and Eeny and Cousin Augustus in the other; Eek had had a headache and Mrs. Bean wouldn't let him come; she had given him a sixteenth of an aspirin tablet and made him go to bed. And Freddy had squealed because Eeny and Cousin Augustus had got to scuffling in his pocket, and they tickled.

But Mr. Flint thought he was afraid. He gave a snort of contempt. "Beat it, peewee."

"There isn't any—" Freddy began, and then, remembering to talk Western, he began again. "That ain't no reason I should beat it, pardner, seein' as I can outride and outshoot you. I wouldn't fight you—it would be plain murder."

"Outride! Outshoot!" Mr. Flint sputtered. "Why, you— Folks!" He turned to the dudes, who were watching with interest. "This here critter—why he ain't even a man, he's nothing but a pig! An educated pig, from down to Bean's place, west of Centerboro. Why—"

"What's the use of calling him names, Mr. Flint?" said Mrs. Balloway. "That doesn't prove anything. Can he outride and outshoot you?"

Freddy swung down from the saddle. "Let's see you fork this bronc, Flint," he said. "Stay on him ten seconds and I'll admit I'm a liar."

"Oh, sure, sure," Mr. Flint said. "When you got him trained to throw anybody off but you? What'll that prove?"

"O K," said Freddy. "Then it's shooting. Set up your tin cans. I understand you're right accurate with your little old popgun."

"Can't see to shoot by moonlight," put in Jasper. He was one of the two cowboys Mr. Flint had working on the ranch as horse handlers.

"Good enough to beat a pig," said Mr. Flint. "Come along folks," he said, turning to the group about the fire; "over to the corral fence."

Chapter 9

The terms of the shooting match were simple.
Four tin cans were put up on posts of the corral. Then when the horses were driven off out
of the way into the smaller corral by the house,
Mr. Flint would ride down past at a distance
of thirty yards and try to shoot the cans off the
posts. He was allowed six shots, and would ride
at a canter. It was a pretty severe test of marks-
manship.

It was a cool clear night. The moon was high

now, and almost bright enough to read by. Certainly it was bright enough to shoot by. Mr. Flint rode to the end of the corral and then with his gun swinging in his hand cantered down once past the posts to get the distance. Then he went back and rode down again, and this time he shot. He fired twice at the first can before he knocked it off the post, but the second and third ones he hit at the first try. With two cartridges left in his gun he fired more carefully at the fourth can and missed; he fired quickly again and knocked it off the post.

The dudes applauded, and Mr. Flint pulled up beside Freddy. "Let's see you tie that, pig."

"I ain't aimin' to tie it, pardner," said Freddy. "That was right good plain shooting, but what I'm aimin' to show you is something real fancy." He started to pick up four more cans from the pile that had been brought out.

"Jasper'll put up the cans for you," said Mr. Flint.

"I'll put 'em up myself," said Freddy. "I've heard of cans bein' fastened down so that they wouldn't fall off if you hit 'em with a cannon." He went over and placed the cans on the posts. And of course on each post he put a mouse.

The mice had been busy, each chewing a wad of gum, and now their job was to stick one end of a piece of string to each can, throw the loose end down, run to the ground, and be ready to pull.

"Now, folks," he said, "this here ain't going to be a real exhibition, because I'm a little out of trainin'. Of course Flint here has done right well for a feller that ain't never practised shootin' off anything but his mouth. I wouldn't say nothing about it, except he's seen fit to call me pigs and such-like. And I still wouldn't say anything about it if I hadn't seen him beating a horse—this horse, folks, which I had to buy it off him to keep him from killing it."

Mr. Flint reined in closer to Freddy. "You keep your mouth shut, you little tramp," he said angrily, "or I'll— Ouch!" he yelled suddenly. For he had forgotten about Cy, who had swung round and nipped him sharply in the leg.

Freddy rode up to the end of the corral. "O K, Cy," he said, and the pony gathered his legs under him and sprang. They came down past the posts at a dead run. As they passed the first post, Freddy didn't shoot, and Jasper said with a chuckle to Mr. Flint, "The dope ain't even got his gun out."

But opposite the second post Freddy snatched his gun from the holster, and as fast as he could pull the trigger fired four shots— bang, bang, bang, bang!—and at each bang a can jumped or toppled from a post. Indeed one of them jumped before the bang came—probably because Cousin Augustus was so excited— but nobody noticed.

The dudes had applauded Mr. Flint, but now they shouted and cheered and crowded around Freddy.

"Shucks," said Freddy, " 'twasn't anything. I just want to show this Mr. Flint why it ain't healthy for him to talk about fighting me. And also and furthermore, I want to help him to keep out of the way of temptation." He rode up closer to Mr. Flint. "Temptation is a terrible bad thing to get into, Mr. Flint," he said. "Like it might be the temptation to rob a bank. You think how nice it would be to have all that money without working for it—just pulling up a trap door and climbing down and scooping it up. But suppose a bullet—like it might be from this gun of mine—comes climbing down after you, hey? Comes right down and pokes its cold nose into your ribs! Hey? You better think it over carefully, Mr. Flint."

"I don't know what you're talking about," said Mr. Flint sullenly.

"Good," said Freddy. "Then there's no harm done. So good evening, folks. Just hand me my guitar, Jasper." He waved his hand and then rode off, stopping opposite the last post of the corral fence where he pretended to tune his guitar while the mice climbed up Cy's foreleg and into his pockets. Then he went on, singing:

"Yippy-i-dee! Yippy-i-day!
Cowboy Bean is coming this way.
He's sharp as a needle and bright as a dollar,
Wears a No. 3 shoe and a 16 collar.
He's full of vim and he's full of vigor,
Fast on the draw and quick on the trigger.
So all you bandits and thieves take warning,
Or you'll be in a hospital bed by morning,
And the doc'll give you kind of a shake,
And he'll hear the rattle that the bullets make,
And he'll shake his head and he'll say: 'O my!
I can't cure this and I ain't going to try,
    Yippy-i-day! Yippy-i-dy!
For Two-Gun Freddy has plugged this guy.'"

Bang-Bang-Bang-Bang!

The other animals were well pleased that Freddy had managed to scare off Mr. Flint. The pig had proved himself such a superb marksman that the ranch owner would hardly dare to try holding up the bank, even with the help of Jasper and Slim. However, Freddy was taking no chances, and the next day when he and his friends were sitting around under the big tree by the back porch, thinking about what they could do to keep an eye on Mr. Flint, Hank said: "What you need is somebody to patrol around the bank nights. Those guards you've got down there, squirrels and like that, they don't stay awake after sundown. Most nights you can hear 'em snorin' half a mile down the road. Anybody could walk right in and go down in the vaults and they wouldn't even turn over on the other side. So I was just wondering—I dunno—but how about getting my friend Sidney to keep an eye on things nights?"

Sidney was a small brown bat who used to come in and flit around and talk to Hank nights when the rheumatism in his off hind leg kept him awake.

"He lives in my barn now," Hank added.

"If you can call it living," said Jinx contemptuously. "Hanging upside down with his eyes shut all day long. Lives on a diet of mosquitoes, so they tell me. And that isn't living either."

"Well, I dunno," said Hank. "I wouldn't care to live on mosquitoes myself. Don't seem as if there's much nourishment in 'em. I guess usually it's t'other way round—what mosquitoes there are here usually live on me. But Sidney keeps 'em cleared out. And why are you so mad because he likes to eat 'em, Jinx?"

"I haven't any use for bats," Jinx said. "Why can't they make up their minds to be either animals or birds—not just stay in between."

"That isn't why you don't like them, though," said Freddy.

"Oh, no? You tell me then."

"Sure, I will. You don't like 'em because they're the one little animal a cat can't catch. They'll outsmart a cat every time."

"Oh, yeah?" said Jinx. "Well, I can make you eat those words, pig, and you'll find them even less nourishing than mosquitoes. I'll go bring Sidney out here to you."

He got up and walked down to the barn. As soon as he had disappeared inside the others got up quietly and sneaked over to where they could see, either through the door or through cracks in the wall, what went on.

Sidney was hanging upside down from one of the beams that supported the floor of the loft. Jinx saw that by standing on a crosspiece that was nailed as a brace between two upright beams against the wall, he could reach up and scoop the bat right down with his paw. Also there was an old stepladder leaning against the wall, and from its top he could jump to the crosspiece.

He went up noiselessly and jumped across. But bats are sensitive to the slightest vibration. Sidney didn't open his eyes, for bats don't depend much on their eyes. He could sense a warm body reaching up towards him, and then when Jinx had stretched up from the crosspiece he dropped, unfolding his wings. Jinx had been hanging on and reaching out with one forepaw; now he let go and snatched with two. But Sidney zigzagged in the crazy way that bats do when they fly, and Jinx missed, lost his balance, and fell splash! into Hank's watering trough. Sidney flew back to the same place and hung himself up and went to sleep again.

The animals came piling into the barn. They tried not to laugh, because they knew Jinx would be pretty sore. And he was, all right. "See what I mean?" he yelled as he climbed out of the trough and shook himself. "See what I mean about bats? Mean, sneaky things! He could dodge me, couldn't he? Didn't have to push me into the trough."

Sidney opened one eye. "Did *not* push him!" he said in the little high squeaky bat's voice. "Why can't you let me alone?" He dropped from the beam and flitted out of the door.

"Now you've done it," said Hank. "He may not come back for a week."

"And good riddance," said Jinx. He was pretty mad. Of course he was really mad at himself because first Howard and then Sidney had got away when he'd tried to catch them. But of course nobody ever admits that he's mad at himself, so Jinx had to just be mad at everybody else. It is not a hard thing to do, though it's sort of foolish, and it usually makes trouble for a lot of innocent bystanders. Jinx glared around at his friends, then he snarled at them and went out into the barnyard.

It was Mrs. Wiggins who found Sidney later

in the day. He was in the cowbarn, hanging upside down against the wall. She told him what the animals wanted.

"Sure, sure!" he said. "I'll keep an eye on your old bank."

"And you'll patrol it nights?"

"I said I would, didn't I?" said Sidney angrily. "What you want me to do—send you a letter about it?"

"I'm sorry to keep you awake when you want to go to sleep," said the cow, "but I have to be sure of your answer, and good land, I can't tell whether you mean it or not when you're looking at me upside down."

" 'Tisn't upside down to me," said the bat.

"Maybe not. But when you're talking to people, their expression is just as important as what they say, and you talk to anybody upside down and their expressions don't mean anything. Your mouth is at the top of your head and if you smile the corners turn down instead of up, and your eyes look funny too. You—"

"Look," Sidney interrupted her. "I said I'd do it. Now just never mind criticizing my features and go on let me sleep, will you."

So Mrs. Wiggins went away. "There's one

thing that bat taught me," she said to Freddy later. "I've never been a good liar. Folks can always tell by my face when I'm lying. Well, next time I want to tell a lie and get away with it, I'm going to stand on my head. Nobody can tell anything by my face then."

Chapter 10

Freddy felt pretty sure that Mr. Flint would have given up any idea he might have had of robbing the bank. At least he wouldn't try it when Freddy was around, for he had seen the pig do some wonderful shooting, and he wouldn't take chances with anything involving gunplay. So for a few days everything was quiet and peaceful. Freddy practised riding and roping; he was getting good enough so that he could have got a job as a cowboy if there had been any demand for them in the neighborhood. He galloped around over the farm, and he roped everything in sight. He got Mrs. Wiggins to help him at first; she would run, and then he would gallop after her and lasso her. But it wasn't much fun for her. When you run and somebody ropes you, you're likely to fall down and skin your nose. After this had happened several times, the cow quit. Indeed she was so lame from falling down that she said she couldn't run once around the barnyard without yelling. She got a bottle of arnica from Mrs. Bean and a bottle of liniment from Mr. Bean and Freddy found a bottle of something Uncle Ben had had, up in the loft. She mixed them all together and rubbed them on, and then she said she felt better. She certainly smelt different.

Every night now the Horrible Ten were out, marching and war-dancing and singing their songs. Rabbits are mild creatures and a good many animals pick on them for that reason. The rabbits were getting their revenge on a lot of animals who had bullied them in the past. They would lie in wait until they caught some animal in the open, and then they would jump up and go through their act. It was a good act, so good that when they had scared all their enemies, they put it on for anybody they happened to run into. They claimed that they had scared one woodchuck so badly that his fur had turned white. But I don't think there was any truth in that.

Jinx liked their act so much that he wanted to join them. But they said no, that would make them the Horrible Eleven, which sounded foolish. Their real reason was that they knew that Jinx, being larger than the others, would want to be the head Horrible and run things. He said he would be a big help to them; first, because he was very good at blood-curdling screams; and second, because if they got in a fight, he could protect them. But they said that while screams would be nice, they'd got along so far without them; and as for protection, they didn't need it, because if an animal got mad and attacked them, they could always run away. And of course a rabbit can run like a streak of greased lightning.

The most successful performance was the night they put their act on for the benefit of Mrs. Wiggins and her two sisters, Mrs. Wurz-

After this had happened several times the cow quit.

burger and Mrs. Wogus. The cows had heard a good deal about the Horrible Ten, but as they seldom went out nights, they had never seen them in action, so they sent them an invitation to come into the cow barn some night and put on their act.

The Horrible Ten accepted, but wouldn't say when they were coming. They wanted to make it a surprise. They did all right. They came in one night during a thunderstorm and war-danced in a circle around the cows, and sang their songs, and the lightning flickered on their tin knives and their rolling eyeballs and made them appear and disappear as they stamped and shouted, and it was pretty terrifying. Mrs. Wurzburger fainted away and Mrs. Wogus got down and hid her head in the hay. Mrs. Wiggins was scared too, but she had a lot of common sense, so she could laugh even when she was scared. When Mrs. Wiggins laughed you could hear her down in Centerboro. The Beans of course heard her and thought she was having hysterics, and Mr. Bean came out with a pail of water and threw it over her. She didn't like that much, but she didn't want Mr.

Bean to get mad at her, so she just thanked him and said she felt better.

The rabbits' friends, however, felt that sooner or later they were going to get into real trouble. They were getting much too bold, and some of their exploits were decidedly foolhardy. They went up in the woods and scared Mac, the wildcat, or at least tried to. Mac snarled and spit at first, but he had heard about the Horribles, and after a minute he calmed down and just grinned at them.

But when Freddy heard about it, he gave No. 23 a good talking to. "You keep this up," he said, "and you won't be the Horrible Ten long. You'll be the Horrible Nine and then the Horrible Eight, and pretty soon the Horrible Nothing. You know perfectly well that a lot of rabbits have gone into those woods and never come out again. Why, last winter your own grandfather disappeared up there. I'm not accusing Mac of eating him. But your grandfather, if I remember correctly, was rather on the plump side. And what do you suppose happens, out in the woods, if a nice plump rabbit comes around one side of a bush and a hungry wildcat comes around the other? You think they just say 'How-de-do?' and pass on?"

"Oh, shucks, Freddy," said No. 23; "you know grandpa was awful slow on his feet. Us Horribles, we're all good runners."

"Have it your own way," said Freddy. "But if you get into trouble, I won't be able to say 'I told you so' but I'll think of you whenever I see Mac. So long, 23; it's been nice knowing you."

But Freddy's warning didn't have much effect.

Every day after breakfast Freddy saddled Cy and rode off, sometimes along the roads, sometimes cross country. Often it was late at night before they got home. The mice enjoyed these rides as much as Freddy did, and he usually took one or two of them along. Even Cousin Augustus, although the motion of the horse usually made him seasick, insisted on going. He groaned and complained all the time, and wasn't a very cheerful companion, but he raised such a rumpus if he was left behind that everybody begged Freddy to take him.

Freddy often met the dudes from Mr. Flint's ranch, and if neither Mr. Flint nor Jasper was along, he would sometimes ride with them a while or accept their invitation to a picnic. None of them knew that he was a pig, although they had all by this time heard of Mr. Bean's talking animals, and one evening around their campfire they started asking him questions about them. Particularly they wanted to know if he had ever seen Freddy, the famous pig detective, who was also a poet.

"Is he really as smart as they say?" someone asked. "I mean, we hear about all these disguises he wears; can he really get away with it?"

"Oh, sure!" said Freddy. "Sure! Why, that pig, he might sit right here 'mongst us—he might be any one of you folks, and there ain't anybody that would guess it. Why, he might even be me!"

They all laughed heartily at this. "Oh, come, come," they said, "we aren't as easy to fool as that!"

That was too much for Freddy. There wasn't any reason why he should keep pretending with these people, he thought, and he snatched off his big hat. "In fact," he said, "he is me. Or at least—I'm him!"

Well, they were all astonished. They had

thought he was a pretty queer-looking cowboy, but it had certainly never occurred to them that he was a pig. They all took it pretty well, because people don't usually like to be made to look foolish, and of course you look pretty foolish if you can't tell the difference between a pig and a cowboy. They crowded round and shook hands and congratulated him on his disguise, and particularly on the way he could ride and shoot. "My gracious," said Mrs. Balloway, "that was the most wonderful exhibition you gave us the other night. You know the rodeo is to be held next week, and I do hope you'll be entered in some of the shooting events."

"There's one shooting event he'll be entered in, all right," said a voice from the darkness, and Jasper rode into the firelight. "Flint's been looking for you, pig. It's just as well for you I got to you first. Because if you run into him you ain't going to get much warning. He's going to shoot on sight."

There was a gasp from the dudes, and one of them said: "Why, he must be crazy! This man —this, er, person can shoot all around Mr. Flint."

"That's just what Cal thinks, ma'am," said

Jasper. "That he'll shoot all around him and won't hit him. Any more than he hit them cans he was shooting at so bold and free."

"But we saw him hit them."

"You thought you saw him hit them. So did I, till we looked at the cans, and there weren't any bullet holes in any of 'em."

"Oh, nonsense!" said Mrs. Balloway. "Why, we saw them knocked off the posts when he fired at them."

"I don't know how he did it—maybe with strings," said Jasper. "But he never hit one of those cans—there ain't a hole in one of 'em."

It hadn't occurred to Freddy that they might look at the cans. It would have been easy enough to puncture them just before putting them on the posts. The dudes were all looking at him. He jammed his hat back on his head and glared angrily at Jasper. "Nonsense!" he said. "You all saw me knock the cans off. How could I do that if I didn't hit them? By magic? Maybe the cans were so scared they jumped right off the posts. Maybe—" He was thinking hard as he talked. He had to face Jasper down on this, otherwise his reputation would be gone. He realized again that a reputation was a nuisance.

Here he was, trying to live up to a reputation as a marksman, and probably a gun fighter, when he had nothing but blanks in his gun, and the only time he had ever shot at a mark, he had missed it by three feet. "I wish I'd stuck to detective work," he thought.

"Well, whether he hit the cans or not," said Mrs. Balloway, "Mr. Flint is talking a lot of foolishness. It may be all right out West where you come from to talk about shooting on sight, but if he tries out any such lawless notions around this part of the country, he'll wind up in jail."

"Ma'am," said Jasper. "If Cal was to pull a gun on a man, without even giving him due warning, I'd agree with you. But this here feller ain't a man, he's a pig. And there wouldn't be any jail sentence for shootin' a pig. Maybe he'd have to pay the pig's owner something. But I guess Cal would think it was worth it." He grinned maliciously at Freddy.

Freddy had by this time recovered himself. He had no desire to be shot up by Mr. Flint, but Mr. Flint was not present. Of course, whatever he said about Mr. Flint would be reported to him, but nothing could make things any worse: Mr. Flint was going to shoot him on sight anyway. So he said boldly: "Jasper, yo' can tell that long-nosed pickle-faced boss of yours that he ain't going to have to hunt for me. I'll be up to the ranch, lookin' for him, and if he comes out, he'd better come out a-shooting. Not that I think he will come out—I reckon I'll have to come in and get him, which I aim to do just that, and I'll pull him out like a robin pulls a worm out of the dirt, and I'll shoot him so full of holes you can set glass in him and use him for a window." And Freddy swung up into the saddle, struck a chord on his guitar, and as he rode off out of the circle of firelight into the darkness, he sang:

"Up to the ranch rides Cowboy Freddy;
His heart is stout and his hand is steady;
He yells: 'Come out' but Flint is yeller
And he shakes and he shivers and he hides in
  the cellar.
  Oh, yip, yip, yippy-doodle-dee!
When Freddy finds him he falls on his knees,
And he says, 'Oh, mercy!' and he says, 'Oh,
  please!'
But Freddy just laughs and pulls his moustache,

And he plugs old Flint in the middle of his
    sash.

  Sing yip, yip, yippy-doodle-do."

There was much more in the song, but there
was a lot of bragging in it, and Freddy was a
little ashamed of it afterwards, so it is not put
down here.

Chapter 11

But Freddy didn't go home that night. He had no wish to be pulled out of his comfortable bed in the pigpen in the middle of the night by an enraged Mr. Flint, and maybe shot full of large round holes. So he rode around the end of the lake to Mr. Camphor's house. He rode up to the front door and rang the bell.

Bannister answered. Bannister was Mr. Camphor's butler, a very tall man in a tail coat with a very high bridge to his nose which he held so high in the air that unless you were an important personage, he could almost never see you over it. Freddy, however, was pretty high up in the air, too, being on horseback, so after Bannister had said: "Sorry, sir, Mr. C. Jimson Camphor is not at home," he caught sight of the pig. "My word," he said, "it is Mr. Frederick! Happy to see you, sir."

"Thank you, Bannister," said Freddy. He pointed to two mice who were peeking out of his pockets. "You remember Cousin Augustus. And this is my friend, Howard. And this pony is another new friend, Cy."

"Happy to see you, gentlemen," said Bannister. "Mr. Camphor is in Washington. He will be sorry to have missed you. But come in, come in. Your room is always kept ready for you, you know, Mr. Frederick. And we can put these two gentlemen in the blue room, I think. As for Mr. Cy—" he looked doubtfully at the horse.

"Cy's a Western pony—never sleeps indoors," said Freddy.

"We'd rather sleep in the kitchen if it's all right," said Cousin Augustus, and Howard said: "We don't feel at home in bedrooms. No crumbs usually."

"Dear me," said Bannister, "two mice with

but a single thought." Then he looked startled. "Ha!" he said. "Ha, ha! I seem to have made a joke!"

Cousin Augustus was offended. "Yeah?" he said. "Well, it doesn't seem very funny to me."

"He's not making fun of you, mouse," said Freddy. "It's just a quotation he's twisted around. It's two *minds* with but a single thought, you know."

"No offense meant," said Bannister.

"O K," said Cousin Augustus grumpily, for he was still a little seasick from the ride. "O K, O K, O K. Well, let him mind his manners and not go throwing his quotations at me."

So they spent a quiet night at Mr. Camphor's, and in the morning they held a council of war, with Bannister's help. There was a good deal of arguing, particularly between Bannister and Cousin Augustus, who still seemed to hold a slight grudge against the butler. But at last a plan was decided on.

That afternoon they paddled across the lake —all but Cy who refused (and I think, on the whole, sensibly) to get into the canoe—and had a picnic at their old camp site on the north shore. And the following morning Bannister drove them into Centerboro, where Freddy bought a number of things. He bought a false moustache and a wig with long hair, that made him look like pictures of General Custer. He bought a green shirt with a design of yellow pistols on it, and a new gun belt studded with what looked like diamonds but probably weren't; and he bought a great many packages of red Easter egg tint. After that they spent nearly a whole day tinting Cy, and turning him from a buckskin into a roan.

Both Cy and Bannister agreed that the plan that Freddy had finally adopted was a very dangerous one, because its success depended on how good his disguise was. And as a rule Freddy's disguises were interesting, but not very convincing. If his moustache fell off, or if his wig slipped sideways, he was sure to be recognized. And if he was recognized, he ran a very good chance of being shot at. But Freddy was determined. He was really quite a courageous pig. I don't mean that he wasn't scared; he was so scared thinking about it sometimes that his teeth chattered and his tail came completely uncurled. But he didn't propose to let being scared interfere with what he intended to do.

And so, after all his preparations were made, on the day of Mr. Flint's rodeo he saddled Cy and they started for the ranch.

Now a good disguise isn't just something you put on, like false whiskers, or a funny hat. You have to take all the little things that people might recognize you by, and change them. And one of the most important of these is the way you walk. For people can recognize you by your walk long before they get close enough to see your face. So Freddy, who ordinarily sat up pretty straight, slouched in the saddle and held his head on one side, and Cy trotted along with a quick little jerky step that was quite unlike his usual gait. From a distance they certainly wouldn't look familiar to Mr. Flint. And when they got closer, Cy's color, and Freddy's long drooping moustache and lank black hair hanging down over his collar, would throw him completely off the track.

Mr. Flint's rodeo was of course a small one, but he had brought along a few animals for the steer-wrestling and calf-roping events, and a few horses that would buck mildly when teased. The prize money he was offering wasn't large, but several riders who had been making the rounds of the eastern rodeos dropped in to try to pick up a little of it. Some bleachers had been knocked together and when Freddy got there there was a good-sized crowd filling the bleachers and strung out along the fence surrounding the arena. A lot of his friends from Centerboro were there. He saw Judge Willey and the sheriff, and Mr. Weezer and old Mrs. Peppercorn.

Freddy rode up to the gate through which the contestants entered just as the calf-roping was over. Mr. Flint had won with a time of twenty seconds, and the audience applauded him as he came out. He stopped as he caught sight of Freddy. I guess you can't blame him, for Freddy, though small, was a pretty tough-looking specimen as he sat there pulling at his long black moustache. He didn't of course pull it very hard, for it was only fastened on with mucilage. One of the dudes, who was familiar with the pictures of the old-time Western bad men, said that he looked like Wild Bill Hickok, seen through the wrong end of a telescope.

"Howdy, mister." Freddy made his voice as hoarse and rough as he could. "You the boss here?"

"That's right," said Mr. Flint. "You want to

get in the show?" Suddenly he turned away from Freddy, to look towards Jasper who had set up a target on one of the corral posts, and was about to give an exhibition of knife throwing. "Jasper," he called, "lay off that till I get around back of the pen."

"I forgot, boss," said Jasper. "Can't stop now; you look the other way." And he pulled out a sheath knife and balanced it on his palm.

Freddy started to say something and then stopped, for Mr. Flint seemed to have been taken suddenly sick. He reached up and took hold of Freddy's saddle horn and supported himself by it as he leaned against Cy. Big drops of sweat ran off his forehead and he shut his eyes and began to tremble. Cy looked around and raised his eyebrows inquiringly, but Freddy shook his head at him warningly. It was a nice chance to take a good bite out of Mr. Flint, but it would spoil their plan.

Jasper held the knife flat, on his open hand, point towards him; then tossed it underhand with a flip, and it turned over twice in the air and went plunk! into the center of the target. And Mr. Flint jerked as if it had gone into him.

"You shore look sick, mister," said Freddy.

"Likely you ought to get in the bunkhouse."

Plunk! went another knife, and Mr. Flint jerked again and moaned faintly, and then Jasper came running over to them. "Get him out of here," he said disgustedly, "I've got to finish this now I've started it. He can't stand knives—makes him sick to see 'em. I guess he cut his finger when he was a little boy or somethin'. Hey, you—Slim!" he called to another puncher, "Get the boss out of here."

Slim came over and said: "Come on, boss," rather contemptuously, and then he hooked Mr. Flint's arm over his shoulder and led him around behind the bleachers.

Freddy watched the knife throwing. Jasper was good. He threw mostly underhand and could make the knife turn over one, two or three times before it hit the target. His final stunt was to throw at a can tossed in the air. He pierced it on the third try.

Freddy waited around. He watched some fancy riding, and after a while Mr. Flint came back. He looked all right.

"Must have et something that disagreed with me," he said. "Now, was you aimin' to get into the show? Good chance to make a little prize money, if you can beat the time of some of these other boys."

Freddy shook his head. "Your money don't interest me none, pardner. Maybe you heard of me; I'm Snake Peters. Come from Buzzard's Gulch, Wyoming. I been sort of sashayin' round mongst these rodeos, tryin' to find somebody could stay on this little horse of mine more'n thirty seconds. You got any good riders?"

"He don't look very tough," Mr. Flint said. Cy certainly didn't. He stood awkwardly with his front feet crossed, and everything about him drooped—his tail, his eyelids, his head; and his mouth was open. He looked worn out and sort of half-witted, if there is such a thing as a half-witted horse. Mr. Flint went up and stroked his neck, then he poked him in the ribs. Cy didn't move.

Mr. Flint shook his head, "We can't use horses like that in our show, friend. Even if you put up money for any rider that could stay on him. We got to give the customers some excitement, and there ain't enough excitement in that animal to put in a bug's ear."

"I've got five dollars for anybody can stay on him thirty seconds," said Freddy.

"Move along, move along," said Mr. Flint irritably. "And take that hunk of crowbait away from here. Go on; beat it."

A number of the onlookers had edged up to listen, and among them was Bannister, who now pushed forward. "I say, hold on a minute," "I'll ride this creature for five dollars. I have never ridden a horse, but if someone will help me up into the saddle I am sure I can stay on thirty seconds."

Mr. Flint started to object, but some of the crowd had begun to laugh, and he hesitated. "Well, O K," he said. "We need a good clown act. Get down you, Peters; and Jasper, get that megaphone and give 'em an announcement."

So Jasper went out in front of the bleachers. "Ladies and gentlemen," he said, "Mr. Snake Peters, the gentleman with the wind-blown bob and the soup strainers, has offered five dollars to anyone who can stay on this here wall-eyed roan horse of his for thirty seconds. His offer has been took up by the gentleman in the clawhammer coat. This gentleman—what's your name? Bannister?—this Mr. Bannister claims he's never rode anything livelier than a wooden horse on a merry-go-round, but in spite of the way Mr. Peters' horse is a-rarin' and snortin' fire, he's going to try for the five dollars."

The bleachers laughed and applauded, and Mr. Flint hoisted Bannister into the saddle, and shoved Cy through the gate. It certainly wasn't much of a show. Cy walked slowly up to the fence, leaned against a post, dropped his head and went to sleep. When Mr. Flint called, "Time!" he woke up, walked back, and Bannister was helped down.

Freddy handed over the five dollars. Then he grabbed the megaphone and before Mr. Flint could stop him, he addressed the crowd. "Ladies and gentlemen, I am now offering Mr. Flint himself fifty dollars if he can stay on my horse thirty seconds." Then, remembering that he was supposed to be a wild and wooly Westerner, he continued: "This here horse, gents and ladies, has got a kind nature. He knowed that this Bannister wasn't a fair match for him, and he let him off easy. But Cal Flint here, he's good, he's—"

"Oh, dry up and get out of the arena," Mr. Flint interrupted. But there were shouts from the bleachers: "Go on, Cal. See if you can wake the old nag up. Ride him, cowboy!" He turned to Freddy. "Let's see the color of your money."

So Freddy pulled out some bills. Mr. Flint looked at them, then swung into Cy's saddle. Jasper held the watch, and when he yelled, "Time!" Mr. Flint jabbed his spurs in and whacked Cy with his hat. But Cy didn't start anything. He just ambled off around the arena, and when Mr. Flint realized that he looked rather foolish yelling and jumping around on such a quiet animal, he relaxed and sat easily in the saddle, dropping the reins and folding his arms. It was then—at the twentieth second —that Cy stumbled. His forefeet stumbled, and at the same time his hindquarters twisted sideways. And Mr. Flint somersaulted right over his shoulder.

He was up in an instant. He paid no attention to the crowd which was staring open-mouthed, but ran after Cy who had trotted back to the gate. "Hey!" he shouted to Freddy. "That wasn't fair—it was an accident! It was a trick! I demand another trial." He grabbed Cy's bridle.

"You're a poor sport, Flint," said Snake Peters, smoothing his long moustache. "You had your trial. You ain't earned your money. 'Tisn't my fault if you can't ride a horse without being

His hindquarters twisted sideways.

tied to the saddle. Stand away from that pony."
He dropped his right hand to the butt of his
gun.

Freddy was sure that Mr. Flint would not
care to put himself in the wrong with the crowd
by shooting, and he was right. The man took his
hand from the bridle. "That was a trick," he
said angrily. "I don't want your money. But I
ain't going to have it said that Cal Flint can't
ride a half-dead old plug that ought to be
shipped off to the boneyard."

"I don't want your money either," said
Freddy. "But you ain't going to get another
trial free." He started to spit out of the side of
his mouth to make himself more like Snake
Peters than ever, but decided against it on account of the moustache. "Lemme see, those are
nice guns you got there. You stay on this horse
thirty seconds and you get fifty dollars, but if
he throws you, I get the guns. Is it a deal?"

"If I can't stay on that camel I'll shoot myself
with those guns," said Mr. Flint. "Sure it's a
deal. Keep the time, Jasper." A second later he
was astride Cy.

When Mr. Flint got into the saddle, Cy woke
up. He woke up so violently that it was as if he

had suddenly exploded. He bucked and whirled, reared up and twisted and put his head down and almost stood on his forelegs. Mr. Flint's arms and legs flew in all directions and his head snapped back and forth until it looked as if it would fly off. He lasted seven seconds. Then he catapulted through the air and smacked flat on his face on the ground, and Cy picked him up in his teeth by the seat of his pants and tossed him over the fence.

The crowd in the bleachers yelled and waved and were so excited that several of them fell between the benches and had to be dragged out from below. Mr. Flint sat up slowly, shook his head several times, then got to his feet.

Freddy came up to him. "I'll take those guns, Flint," he said.

Mr. Flint glared at him viciously. He pulled out the guns, and for a minute Freddy thought that he was a gone pig. But Jasper had hold of Mr. Flint's arm. "Easy, boss," he said. "Don't let the crowd get sore on you." And he took the guns from him. Then he turned to the bleachers. "Mr. Flint wants me to say," he called, "that he's paying up because he lost the bout, according to the terms as they was arranged. But he also wants me to say that what you have just seen here is not a straightforward performance. This horse is not the usual wild horse used in such trials. He's a trick horse, trained to throw you off your guard and then cut loose on you. He wants me to say—"

The crowd began to jeer. "Yah! He lost, didn't he? Why don't he shut up?"

Freddy had got into the saddle, and he now rode up towards the bleachers. So far everything had gone as he had hoped. He had disarmed Mr. Flint; now, in front of all the people, dudes from the ranch and neighbors from Centerboro and the surrounding farms, he planned to stand up and tell his story. He was going to take off his disguise and then, holding the guns on Flint to keep him from interfering, he was going to tell of Mr. Flint's cruelty to Cy, of his plan to rob the Animal Bank, and of his threat to shoot him, Freddy, on sight. For he believed that to get his story before the public was the only way to protect himself from being killed. The anger of the whole community, Freddy thought, turned against Mr. Flint, would make him behave himself.

Now this was not a bad plan. If nobody knew

about his threat, Mr. Flint could shoot Freddy and pretend that it was an accident. But if everybody knew about it, he couldn't make the accident story stick. Everybody would be pretty mad at Mr. Flint, for Freddy was a popular pig, not only among the animals, but among the Centerboro people.

Unfortunately, just as Jasper turned to hand the guns to Freddy, a little gust of wind came along. It swirled around Freddy, lifted the brim of his hat, twisted his moustache, lifted the long hair of the wig that hung over his shoulders. Mr. Flint was looking at him, and suddenly he recognized him. He gave a yell and grabbed the guns back from Jasper. "The pig!" he shouted. "Draw, pig, defend yourself!"

This time Freddy just about gave up hope. The guns were within a foot of his stomach, and he could feel his stomach trying to sneak around and hide behind his backbone. Jasper said: "Hey! Hey, boss; don't do it!" But Freddy could see that nothing was going to stop Mr. Flint this time. Bannister had come through the gate and was trying to get round behind Mr. Flint, but Freddy knew that he would be too late.

And then Howard climbed up out of Freddy's pocket and did one of the bravest deeds ever done by any mouse in the history of the world. He jumped to one of the pistol barrels, ran up the arm to the shoulder, and dove right down the open collar of Mr. Flint's shirt.

Mr. Flint gave a yell and threw up his arms, and then as Howard galloped around inside his shirt, tickling his ribs, he danced and squirmed and slapped himself, and finally lay down and rolled on the ground. The people on the bleachers thought he had gone crazy, of course, and Jasper kept dancing around him and saying: "Hey, boss! For goodness' sake! What's got into you? Hey, quit it; they're all looking at you!" He was plainly ashamed of Mr. Flint's behavior.

After a minute Mr. Flint stopped and sat up, for Howard had managed to sneak out again down one sleeve, and had run through the grass to where Bannister was standing and climbed up into his pocket. Mr. Flint looked around in a dazed way, then suddenly leaped to his feet, snatched up the guns he had dropped, and ran for his horse. "Jasper!" he shouted. "You fool, you let that pig get away. Come on!" For

Freddy, on his dyed pony, was galloping off across the fields towards the woods.

The first few minutes of the chase were the worst for Freddy, because it was in those minutes that Mr. Flint almost caught up. His tall bay horse was faster than Cy, but Cy was a better jumper and quicker at dodging obstructions. Freddy gave Cy his head, and the pony sailed over walls and ditches, and the pig stuck to his back as if he was glued on, although at the third wall his hat had flown off and he had nearly gone after it, trying to catch it. But he had certainly learned to ride. At each jump Mr. Flint lost ground, gaining it again on the open stretches. But pretty soon they got into rougher going on the edge of the woods—a pasture studded with big boulders and half overgrown with spiny thorn brush—and here Mr. Flint began to fall farther and farther behind. He had fired two or three times, but the bullets had gone wide, and at last he gave up and waited for Jasper to overtake him. They sat staring for a few minutes after the escaping pig, then turned back towards the ranch.

Chapter 12

None of Freddy's friends in the bleachers had
recognized him, so naturally the crowd thought
this was all part of the show. It didn't make
much sense, but then, lots of the movies they
went to in Centerboro didn't make much sense
either, so they just thought maybe they had
missed something, and it would be explained
later. But Jasper and Mr. Flint came back and
at once started doing stunts with a bull whip,

and a rope, and pretty soon the crowd forgot, although some of them wondered why, if Snake Peters was part of the show, he didn't come back.

Bannister didn't stay any longer. He got in his car and drove Howard back to the Bean farm. Mr. and Mrs. Bean had hitched Hank up to the buggy and gone to visit Mrs. Bean's aunt for a few days, but all the other animals were there, and in a meeting in the cow barn Bannister told them what had happened. When he spoke of Howard's heroic attack on Mr. Flint, they cheered until the windows rattled, and even Charles admitted that, except for himself, he knew very few animals who would have dared to perform such a brave deed.

Mrs. Wiggins said that one thing seemed plain: they would have to get rid of Mr. Flint. "If it was just the bank," she said, "I guess we could manage. We could move all our valuables to some other place until his season at the ranch is over and he goes away. But he's out to get Freddy, and sooner or later he'll succeed unless something is done. I wish Freddy was here; he's always so full of ideas."

"I guess his idea today wasn't so hot," said

Jinx. "A couple more like that and there'll be a pig pen to rent."

"I gathered," said Bannister, "that it was the only idea he had at the time, and he thought it better to use a poor one than none at all."

During the discussion several of the rabbits had got up and gone quietly out, and now No. 23 came back with a folded paper which he laid down in front of Howard.

"What's this?" said the mouse. "For me?"

"Sure; open it, open it," said the rabbit.

"Let me open it for you," said Bannister. So Howard got up on the butler's shoulder, and Bannister unfolded the paper. It was a piece of a paper bag, and the writing on it had evidently been done with a very hard pencil by a very poor writer. "My word," said Bannister, "can you read this?"

Like most field mice Howard had had no schooling and could neither read nor write, but he was ashamed to say so at a meeting of such highly educated animals, so he said: "Please read it out loud."

"The writing is so faint," said Bannister, "that I think it is meant to be read in a whisper. But if you say so—" And he read:

"Honorable Howard,

Respected Sir:

Whereas, in the endeavor to save the life of our mutual friend and comrade, Freddy, you boldly and without hesitation risked your own life by leaping into the very lion's jaws (i. e., Mr. Flint's shirt);

And whereas, you thus exhibited a gallantry of conduct far in excess of the line of duty;

Be it therefore resolved that you be invited to join this organization, with the rank of Associate Horrible, and with all the rights and privileges thereto appertaining.

Signed, for the Horrible Ten
Twenty-three, Head Horrible."

There was renewed cheering and calls for a speech.

"Oh dear," said Howard, "I can't make a speech."

"Have to," said Bannister. "There's nothing to it, really. They don't expect an oration. Just say anything that comes into your head."

"The only thing that comes into my head is, I wish they'd shut up."

"Can't say that, naturally," said Bannister. "Oh, just use one of the stock openings. You know! 'Unaccustomed as I am to public speaking,' and so on. Or: 'You'd scarce expect one of my age to speak in public on the stage.' Well, come on, you've got to say something."

So Howard said: "Ladies and gents—I mean, animals and birds. I want to thank the Horribles for their kind invitation. I mean—well, I'll try to be a good member and be as horrible as possible. I guess Mr. Flint thought I was horrible when I was running around over his ribs." He hesitated a minute and then said: "Well, I guess that's all," and crept down into Bannister's pocket.

Bannister had never heard of the Horrible Ten, and so No. 23 said he would show him who they were. All the rabbits went out and got their knives and tied down their ears, and then Mrs. Wiggins turned out the electric light so that the moonlight that came through the windows just showed up things dimly. And then the Horribles came in. They hopped and stamped in a circle around Bannister, and they sang:

"Oh, here we are back again,
The horrible, Horrible Ten,
More horrible than ever,
It's our conscientious endeavor

To catch a butler once a week,
To tie him up and make him squeak,
We make him squeak and we make him squeal
As we chop him up for our evening meal.
And since Bannister's a butler, he
Had better beware of our cutlery,
For it's getting late, and this time of night
We always have a good app—"

The Horribles stopped suddenly, for from somewhere overhead a soft dark object had fallen with a plop to the floor. And then a harsh voice from a beam above them said: "Turn on the light! Quit this foolishness and look what I've brought you. Found it up in that pasture by Flint's ranch."

The light clicked on, and they all looked up to see Old Whibley perched on the beam. His feathers were ruffled and although owls always look worried, he looked much worrieder than usual.

"Look at it! Look at it!" he said crossly. "Don't stand there gaping like a lot of astonished bullfrogs!"

"Why, it's Freddy's hat!" said Robert.

"Look what's in it," said the owl.

"Well," said Jinx, "it hasn't got Freddy in it, so what's all the excitement about?"

"It's got two holes in it," said Whibley. "And if Freddy was in it when those holes were put there, maybe you smart animals can figure out for yourselves where Freddy is now."

Nobody said anything. They all gathered round and looked at the hat, and it was plain enough that a bullet had gone through the hat, and that if Freddy had been wearing it, the bullet had gone through Freddy. Bannister had told them how Mr. Flint and Jasper had chased Freddy up into the woods, shooting at him. And of course none of them knew how the shot Mr. Bean had fired at the side of the pigpen had really made the holes in the hat. Freddy hadn't told them about it, and none of them had noticed the holes.

Whibley clicked his beak irritably. "Come on, come on!" he said. "What do you expect it to do—get up and dance for you?"

But the animals were so shocked that they still couldn't do anything but stare at the hat. That their old friend, Freddy, the cleverest animal on the farm, had been shot, was news so bad that they couldn't take it in. It was Alice,

"Why, it's Freddy's hat!"

the white duck, who broke the spell. She gave a weak quack and fell over in a dead faint.

Alice had come to the meeting with her sister, Emma, and her Uncle Wesley, a pompous little fat duck whom nobody liked. In an emergency Uncle Wesley was no good at all, though he always had a great deal to say. He was cross at Alice for fainting. "Now, now, my girl," he said; "none of that. Come, come; straighten up. At least try to act like a lady—"

"She's fainted, uncle," said Emma. "We must get her out into the air. Take her other wing."

"And don't talk like a fool, Wesley," put in Whibley, "even though you are one. Well now," he said when Alice had been helped out, "I'm asking again, what are you animals going to do?"

It was at times like this that Charles usually leaped up and made a speech, but for once he seemed to have nothing to say. It was Mrs. Wiggins who spoke. "There's only one thing to do," she said. "We're going up and tear Flint's place to pieces, and him with it."

"Right!" said Charles. It was the shortest remark he had probably ever made. And there was a murmur of agreement from the others as they moved towards the door.

But Old Whibley hooted angrily at them. "Sure. That's the thing to do! Walk right up and ask Flint to shoot you. He's got guns. He'll accommodate you, all right. Don't be a set of dim-witted dodunks! Come back here and decide on something sensible."

They stopped and turned around, and Mrs. Wiggins said: "I guess you're right. We can't fight him. But if he's done anything to Freddy—"

There were threatening growls from the animals—even the rabbits tried to snarl, though rabbits haven't anything to snarl with.

Whibley ruffled his feathers and stamped on the beam with irritation. "A plan, we want a plan," he shouted. "We don't want a lot of growls. You can stand there growling at Flint for the next week and how much harm will that do him? Mr. Bean's famous talking animals!" he said sarcastically. "Sure! They can talk but they can't think. All they can do is stand around and cackle like a lot of old hens."

Charles got angry. He strutted out under the beam and shook out his handsome tail feathers.

"Sir," he said, "are you referring by any chance to my wife?"

But Henrietta pushed him aside. "Shut up, Charles," she said, "I'll take care of any personal remarks." And she looked up at the owl. "You're all hoot and hustle, aren't you, old pop-eyes?" she said. "No cackle to you, is there? —just fine common sense and good judgment. Well, you're so much smarter than we are, suppose you tell us what *your* plan is?"

Whibley didn't have any more plan than the others did, but he really was smarter than they were, for he didn't mind admitting it. "Haven't any plan and you know it," he said gruffly. "Didn't intend any personal remark. Just want to get a discussion going. Maybe we can hammer out a plan."

"Excuse me," said Howard, "but I have an idea!"

"Who's this little squirt?" Whibley demanded.

The owl was always offending somebody by his rough speech. Now it was Jinx who got mad. "He's a friend of mine," he said. "And if he's a squirt, you're a moth-eaten old dust mop, and I wouldn't—"

"Now, Jinx," said Mrs. Wiggins reprovingly. "This is just holding everything up." She looked at the owl. "Howard is one of us," she said, "and the only one who appears to have any ideas. Suppose we hear him."

"Quite right," said Whibley. "Speak up, boy, and don't mumble."

"I don't know how to mumble," said Howard, "but I only got as far as the second grade. I just wanted to say that—well, I know one thing that Flint is afraid of, and that's knives." And he told them about what had happened at the rodeo and what Cy had said about it. "And you notice he doesn't wear a knife ever, or carry one."

"That is all true," put in Bannister. "I saw it myself. The fellow turned absolutely green."

"H'm," said Whibley. "His complexion is sort of green anyway. Well, young mouse, your suggestion is that we should attack Flint with knives? And what will he be doing meanwhile?"

"No, sir," said Howard, "I was just thinking that—well, these Horribles have knives. And they don't have to stick them into Flint, if they could just catch him alone—"

"Scare him to death, that's an idea!" said Mrs. Wurzburger.

The owl shook his head. "Not much use scaring Flint," he said. "Scare the dudes that are boarding there—that's the ticket. If they leave, Flint has to close up and go away."

"He's shot Freddy," said Mrs. Wiggins. "We aren't just going to drive him away."

"No," said Old Whibley slowly. "We're going to do more to him than that. But that would be a nice start. See here, you rabbits—what do you call yourselves—Horribles?—could you do a dangerous job? I mean, tackle Flint some night at a campfire, in front of his whole crowd. Of course my niece, Vera, and I would be there—swoop down and grab his guns if he pulled 'em."

Rabbit No. 23 stepped forward. "Brother Horribles," he said, "you have heard the proposal. What do you say?"

There was a shout of: "Yes! Yes, Your Dreadfulness!"

"Especially if Old Whibley and Vera are there," said No. 7. "We know they'd protect us."

"Why, h'm—ha," said the owl, trying not to

look pleased, "good of you to say so. Ha! Where was I? Well, now—"

But a loud "Psst!" from Jinx interrupted him. "Lights out! Horses coming!"

And indeed they could all hear them now, cantering down through the pasture.

Chapter 13

The lights went out just as two horses were
pulled up outside with a scraping of hoofs.
There was a creak of leather, and then foot-
steps, and Mr. Flint came into the barn.

The animals kept still as he peered around.
The moonlight coming through the door and
windows was enough to show him the three
cows, standing placidly chewing away on their
cuds with their backs to him.

"That pig in here?" he said. And then as no

one answered: "Well, speak up! You're Bean's talking animals, ain't you? Let's hear some talk."

There was silence. The cows went on munching.

"Talk, confound you!" the man shouted suddenly. "Where's that pig?" And he lifted the heavy Mexican quirt he was holding, evidently intending to cut Mrs. Wurzburger across the back.

Now Mrs. Wiggins had a little mirror nailed to the wall in front of her. She didn't have it there to admire herself in, for as she said, "I know what I look like, and it's no special pleasure to keep being reminded of it." But she always stood with her back to the door, and this made it possible for her to see who came in before they knew she'd seen them. "And this gives me a little extra time to think up something clever to say to them," she explained. "Not," she added, "that I have ever really managed to do it. But I keep on trying."

So now she saw what Mr. Flint was up to. And as he raised his arm she swung her tail around hard, so that the tuft at the end caught him smack in the face.

His arm dropped and he said "Pffffth!" and backed away. "You stupid brute!" he said, and raised the quirt again, but thought better of it and put it down.

"All right," he said, "so you won't talk, hey? Well, I haven't time to make you." He peered around, and then became aware that there were a great many animals just sitting there in the half darkness, looking at him. He didn't like that much, and since he could see that neither Freddy nor Cy was there, he backed towards the door, dropping his hand to his gun. "No pig here, Jasper," he called. "We'll go on down to the bank. And if you're smart," he said, again addressing the animals, "you'll stay right here and not interfere with us. Shucks," he said, "Animals don't need money. They ain't got any *right* to money. That's what burns me up —that pig, talking as if he was people, with money in the bank and all." He stopped. "Well, never mind that," he said. "And just to show you who's runnin' things, and what you'll get if you monkey with Cal Flint—" He stopped and raised the quirt to slash at Mrs. Wiggins.

"All right, boys," said Old Whibley, and he dropped from the beam and his big talons

Mr. Flint had been butted by Bill.

snatched the quirt from the man's hand. At the same moment Bill and the two dogs jumped, the cows whirled round with lowered horns, and the smaller animals dodged in to do their share. In less time than it would have taken Cy to throw an experienced bronco buster, Mr. Flint had been butted by Bill, and had fallen on his face. Then while Mrs. Wogus, who was the heaviest of the three cows, held him down by sitting on him, the dogs tugged the guns out of his holsters.

Of course the animals could have torn Mr. Flint to pieces. Had they been wild animals, they would probably have done so. But they were all domestic animals—with the exception of Sniffy Wilson, the skunk, and the rabbits and squirrels and chipmunks; and although they had no use for Mr. Flint, they couldn't bring themselves to be very ferocious.

Mrs. Wogus jounced up and down a couple of times to flatten Mr. Flint out good, and with every jounce the air went out of his lungs with a Whoosh! Then she got up, and the Horrible Ten, who had been whispering excitedly in a corner, trooped over. They surrounded Mr. Flint, who had sat up slowly, groaning and rubbing his stomach, and went into their war dance.

They hadn't had time to make up a song, so they just stamped around and waved their knives and gave little yelps, and now and then one of them would think of something and would sing it.

"Flint! Flint!
You're going to be skint,"
                was one of them. And another was:
"See our knives flicker and see our knives flash!
We're going to have us some cowboy hash!"

The performance certainly terrified Mr. Flint. He lay right down on his face and covered his head with his hands and shivered. Jasper, who was beginning to wonder what was going on in the barn, stepped inside the door. "Hey, boss," he began. And then he said: "Whoosh!" in just the same tone that Mr. Flint had said it in, only louder, and he sat down hard, for Bill had butted him square in the middle of the stomach. Then he picked himself up and got on his horse and rode off home.

After a few minutes Old Whibley said: "O K,

boys; don't tire yourselves out," and the Horribles stopped dancing. Then nobody said anything for a while.

By and by Mr. Flint stopped shivering. He lifted his head a little and peeked out with one eye. He saw only the cows, still standing quietly chewing their cuds. And very slowly he got up. Then he started to look for his guns, but Old Whibley's deep voice stopped him. "Get on your horse, Flint."

The man hesitated, but a little voice squeaked:

"Flint! Flint!
You're going to be skint!"

He gave a start, then went straight out and got into the saddle and rode off after Jasper.

"Don't think he'll try the bank tonight," said Whibley. "But just in case he does, I'll take these guns and go down there. When Sidney reports, tell him I'm down there."

With a gun in each strong claw, the owl, flapping hard with his wings—for they were a heavy weight for even so large a bird—flew off into the night.

"You know," said Jinx, "Whibley's a wise old bird, but I think he missed a bet there. We all did."

"I agree with you," said Bannister, coming out from behind the barrel where he had been hiding. "I hope you will not think I am intruding if I suggest that the whereabouts of Mr. Frederick, whether punctured or unpunctured, is the important fact."

"His whereabouts?" asked Mrs. Wogus. "You mean those leather pants he wears over his dungarees? I should think it was Freddy himself we'd want to know about."

"You can't say 'whereabouts *is*,'" said Robert, the collie.

"By 'whereabouts,' madam," said Bannister, "I mean merely his present location. I think therefore, Mr. Robert, that 'is' is the correct form of the verb."

"Don't agree," said Robert shortly. " 'Whereabouts' is plural."

"Who ever heard of one whereabout!" said Bannister.

"Oh, quit wrangling!" said Jinx. "I don't care whether he wore whereabouts or pink suspenders. The point is: if Flint shot Freddy, why did he come here looking for him? We ought to have tied up Flint and questioned him. But maybe the best thing anyway is to go look for him. And for Cy. How come Cy disappeared, too?"

"I just thought," said Howard— "Excuse me, but I just thought; you know Freddy could have stuck his hat up on a stick to draw Flint's fire. That would explain the holes. Maybe Freddy wasn't shot at all."

"No," said Bannister, "that won't work. Freddy was riding hard, and they were riding after him, shooting, when they disappeared up towards the woods. He didn't have time to get behind something and stick up his hat."

"Well, there's something queer about all this," said Mrs. Wiggins, and she backed out of her stall. "Jinx, you and the smaller animals better stay here and look after the house. You know we promised the Beans we'd take care of things, and tomorrow's the day to wind up the clocks. And the squirrels must dust in the parlor in the morning. Robert and Georgie better come with me; we'll see if we can pick up Freddy's trail. Perhaps Bannister would drive us up as far as the spot where Freddy was last seen." Mrs. Wiggins was like most cows, rather quiet and retiring. She seldom put herself forward. But when she did take charge of things, nobody ever opposed her. Probably it was because she never acted until she was sure she was doing the right thing. As I have said before, she had common sense.

Fifteen minutes later Bannister's car, with the butler at the wheel, the dogs beside him, and Mrs. Wiggins in the back seat, was rolling out of the gate. And it would have been two minutes instead of fifteen, only it had taken thirteen minutes of shoving and pulling, of pausing for breath, and of going at it again, to get the cow through the car door.

Chapter 14

Bats are not very sociable animals. It is very difficult to get acquainted with them, but once you have succeeded in winning their friendship they will stick to you through thick and thin. Most animals of course won't take the trouble, since bats sleep all day, and if you want to talk to them you have to sit up half the night. But Hank didn't sleep very well, because his rheumatism bothered him, and so after Sidney had

waked up and had his evening meal of mosquitoes and other small bugs, the two of them had
had long discussions on all sorts of subjects.
They got on well, because while Sidney had a
very strong opinion on almost any subject you
could mention, Hank was always undecided
about everything, and although he never quite
agreed with you, he never quite disagreed
either. So their discussions never turned into
fights.

Sidney knew that he was protecting Hank's
property when he was guarding the bank, so he
did the best job he knew how. Every fifteen
minutes or so he would flit in his crazy zigzag
flight up the road a quarter of a mile and then
circle back around over the fields, and then
after looking in the window to see that the
squirrel guards weren't asleep, would hang up
in the tree by the alarm bell and rest.

It was that same night, on one flight, that he
saw Jasper gallop away from the farm. But once
off the Bean property, the man turned in
among some trees and waited, and pretty soon
Mr. Flint came along and joined him. Sidney
hooked onto a limb over their heads and listened.

Mr. Flint said angrily: "I don't know what I pay you for, Jasper. The minute those critters pitched into me you turned around and beat it."

"I didn't beat it till that goat knocked the wind out of me," said Jasper. "I ain't much good in a fight if I can't breathe. And I knew they wouldn't do anything to you much. That's why I waited. We can go down to the bank now. Could have gone there in the first place if you weren't so set on shootin' that pig. What do we care about the pig? What we want is the money."

"I'll get that pig if it's the last thing I do!" said Mr. Flint vindictively. "Well, O K. We better walk down. Cut the bell rope and then climb down that hole and get the money. I been inquirin' around Centerboro—that pig's well off! They say he even owns some property—a couple of houses. Can you beat it? How'd you like a pig for a landlord?"

Sidney had heard enough. He dropped from the branch. But as he spread his wings to flutter away he had to pass between the two men. Jasper ducked, but Mr. Flint made a quick swipe at him with the quirt, which he had managed to snatch up when he left the barn. Just the tip of it clipped Sidney across the face. Even though he was partly stunned he managed to keep flying, for he knew that if he fell, Mr. Flint would probably hit him again.

"Bats!" Mr. Flint exclaimed. "How I hate the nasty things!"

"You do, hey?" Sidney said to himself as he flew off. "All right, mister; I'll give you bats! But first I'll warn the farm."

So he flew down to the barn, and when he had warned what animals were left there of the danger to the bank, he flew up to the Big Woods, to the old abandoned Grimby house, in the attic of which lived a large colony of bats, most of whom were related to him on his mother's side, his father having come from Connecticut.

In the meantime Mr. Flint and Jasper had crept down close to the bank. The three squirrels on guard inside heard nothing; they were playing dominoes on the trap door that gave entrance to the vaults. Mr. Flint climbed into the tree and cut the alarm bell cord with a small pair of blunt-nosed scissors—he did not, of course, carry a knife, and he wouldn't let

Jasper use his, because the sight of it might make him faint. Then they started around to the front door.

Old Whibley had seen them. The owl was in a spot. He couldn't perch anywhere because he had a gun in each claw and consequently had nothing to perch with. He had been flying round and round above the bank, getting more and more tired—for the guns were heavy. As soon as they came out into the moonlight before the bank door, he aimed one gun and pulled the trigger.

The big Colt .45 went off with a boom that started a lot of things. It broke up the domino game, and the alarmed squirrels made a dash for the bell cord, with the result of course that the cut end came through the hole in the roof when they pulled, and they fell in a heap. Up by the farm the animals, just starting out, broke into a run. And Peter, the bear, who was asleep on the mossy bank by the pool in the woods where Freddy sometimes went to write his poetry, sat up and rubbed his eyes, and then started sleepily down towards the farm.

A .45 kicks hard when it is fired. When Whibley pulled the trigger, the recoil knocked him into a somersault in the air, and he dropped the second gun. When with a good deal of flapping he had recovered himself, he looked down. Mr. Flint was just getting up on one knee from where he had fallen to the ground, and Jasper was running for cover.

"Poor shot," he said disgustedly. "Must have just nicked him." So he fired again.

As a matter of fact he had not nicked Flint; the bullet had gone into the ground ten yards off. What had knocked Flint down was the gun that the owl had dropped.

Flint saw this gun, snatched it up, and he too ran for cover just as the second bullet sang off into the sky. It had been even a worse shot than the first one. Fortunately for Whibley, the gun that Flint had recovered had bounced off his shoulder and fallen so that the barrel was clogged with soft dirt. Flint was afraid that if he fired it before it was cleaned it might explode. Moreover, being fired at from the sky had scared him.

Whibley couldn't see either of the men now. As he circled above the trees he could hear them talking.

"Better make a break for the horses," said

Mr. Flint. "They maybe got a machine gun in that little airplane."

"Airplane, your grandmother's wooden leg!" said Jasper disgustedly. "It's a bird of some kind."

"Who ever heard of a bird shootin'?"

"Who ever heard of a pig ridin' horseback? Shut your eyes a minute, Cal, I see the critter."

There was a pause, and then the owl saw something flying towards him that flashed in the moonlight.

Old Whibley wasn't much good at shooting on the wing, but he had a quick eye, and he made a grab with one claw and caught the knife. He banked, and with a twist of his strong leg, sent it flying back into the shadows where it had come from.

There was a squeal from Mr. Flint, and for a second time the owl thought: "I got him!" But it was the sight of the knife flashing past his nose that had terrified the rancher. He broke from cover and ran for his horse, and after a minute Jasper followed him.

Old Whibley waited a minute to exchange a word with Jinx, and Bill, Mrs. Wiggins' two sisters and several smaller animals who came pelting up the road from the barn. Then he flew after the men. He caught up with them at the edge of the Big Woods and threw a couple more shots after them, and then he stopped and swung up to a high limb and perched. For out of the woods came pouring a cloud of bats.

"Good gracious!" said Old Whibley. "Must be Sidney's mother's folks. Didn't know there were so many of 'em."

As a matter of fact there weren't. But it happened that Sidney's call for help had come just on the night when they were having a family reunion, and aunts and uncles and cousins and children from all over the county had come on for the celebration. Even some bats who were no relation at all had heard about it and had come along, feeling sure that they would have a good time, and that they could claim to be a third cousin of Uncle Jeffrey's wife or something like that, and nobody would know the difference. Hardly anybody keeps track of all the relatives in a family that size.

So the bats had been delighted with the chance to have a little fun, and they came tossing and fluttering out from among the trees, turning and zigzagging and drifting like autumn leaves in a high wind, and chittering happily in their little high voices. When they got near the two horsemen they began flying in a circle around them, a wide one at first, then closer and closer; they dodged the men, who were swinging their hats to drive them off, but they flicked at the horses with their leathery wings, flew under them, grazed their legs and their noses. No horse can stand that sort of thing very long. They began to rear and kick; Mr. Flint's horse lay down and rolled and Mr. Flint had to jump clear; and Jasper got bucked off and fell sprawling. Then the horses ran away.

The two men beat the air with their hats, and the bats continued to circle just out of reach. The sky seemed full of bats, weaving in and out, flying in all directions, but always, as soon as the men dropped their arms to rest, coming in closer, to flick at the uncovered heads with their wings, which made a continuous rustling sound.

The men were getting scared. "What are we going to do?" said Mr. Flint. "I never see bats act this way."

Jasper made another futile swipe with his hat. "Maybe they smell something on us they

No horse can stand that sort of thing very long.

want. Like that pinto of mine'll go through my pockets for sugar. You got any candy in your pocket?"

"Don't be a fool," said Mr. Flint. "Bats don't eat candy. Ain't there anything we can crawl under?"

The bats weren't really doing the men any harm. But there is something ghostly about these animals; they go with witches and broomsticks, and queer sounds in the night, and Hallowe'en. And both Jasper and Mr. Flint were getting good and scared. They went stumbling along, panting and swatting with their hats, and not realizing that the bats were driving them, herding them back down along the edge of the woods—for they couldn't see where they were going; there was nothing to see but the dim flickering of bats' wings wherever they looked.

And then the bats swirled upward and circled above their heads, and they saw that they were surrounded by animals. For the farm animals had followed them.

Mr. Flint looked around at them. There were two cows and a goat and several skunks and a black cat . . . "A cat!" he exclaimed, and stepped towards Jinx, drawing back one foot for a kick.

"Hold it, boss," said Jasper warningly. And as Mr. Flint paused: "Look behind you."

Mr. Flint turned, and there, practically leaning over his shoulder was Peter, the big black bear. "Good evening," said Peter politely.

"Oh," said the man wearily, "I just give up!"

Jinx stepped forward. "Listen, Flint," he said. "This is the last warning you get. You lay off our bank. If you don't—well, first those bats will go up and scare all your boarders so they'll leave. That will ruin your business. But of course, there'll still be you left. And then Peter here will come up to call on you some night and give you a nice hug. Show him, Pete; give him a little hug to show him how we love him."

So Peter put his big forepaws around Mr. Flint's shoulders and squeezed a little, and pretended to kiss Mr. Flint on the top of the head, and Mr. Flint said: "Arrrrh!" and when the bear let go he dropped like a wet dishrag.

Jinx went over and looked at him. "I guess you squoze kind of hard, Pete," he said, "You must be fonder of him than I thought." Then he said, "O K, boys and girls, let's go home. Sidney, you can call off your army."

Mr. Flint got slowly to his feet, and leaning on Jasper's arm he started off towards the ranch. The bats, in little groups, began flying back into the woods. But a dozen or so of Sidney's nearest relatives still circled above the animals, and then one by one peeled off, dove, and buzzed the cat. For Sidney hadn't forgotten Jinx's effort to capture him. Bats hold a grudge a long time; their memory is longer than elephants'.

After five or six of these dives Jinx gave an angry screech and streaked for home.

Chapter 15

When Freddy escaped from Mr. Flint, he didn't go back home, for he had begun to realize what a vindictive nature the man had, and he thought he had better go into hiding for a while. Some time, he knew, he would have to settle with Flint, but he would have to wait until he could think out a good plan. He swung around down into Centerboro and he and Cousin Augustus—for the mouse of course was still in his pocket—rode into the handsomely landscaped grounds of the county jail, which was in charge of his friend, Sheriff Higgins.

The sheriff was at the front door, saying good-bye to a prisoner, Red Mike, whose sentence had just expired. All the other prisoners were there; they had all bought going-away presents for Mike, and Mike had his arms full of them. One of them was a cake with thick chocolate frosting, and the inscription on it in pink: "To Centerboro's most popular criminal. Come back soon, Mike." With all these presents in his arms, Mike was unable to wipe his eyes, out of which tears were trickling, for he had been very happy in the jail.

"Well, Mike," the sheriff said, "we are happy to have had you with us, and if you come back, we will have a big celebration. Of course, I can't *ask* you to try to come back, because that would be askin' you to commit another crime, and that would be a crime in itself—compoundin' a felony and bein' accessory before the fact and I don't know what all. Of course they couldn't put *me* in jail for it, because I'm here already. But they might put me *out* of the jail, which would be worse.

"And I ought to tell you boys," he went on, addressing the others, "that there's been some criticism in town of the way I handle things here. Folks say I'm too good to you boys, that lots of you do wrong just so you can get back here, and that I'm causin' a crime wave in these parts. So I'm askin' you when you're out around town, don't talk too much about the good times we have. Tell 'em I'm a hard man—rule you with an iron hand—that sort of thing. And Mike, don't go showin' that cake around town either. If folks see that—" He broke off as Freddy rode through the gate. "Well, now what in tarnation's this a-comin'?"

Freddy had thought that with his hat gone, he would be easily recognized. But the wig and the moustache changed him so completely that the crowd at the door just stared, and most of them grinned. Freddy stopped, and sat there, pulling his moustache.

"Howdy, gents," he said. "Sheriff, I'm Snake Peters, from Squealin' Snake, Wyoming. Been visitin' the rodeos at some of these Eastern dude ranches, pickin' up a little change doggin' steers and such. Well, sir, this mornin' I'm joggin' along easy, headin' west—I been to this rodeo up to Flint's—when I see two fellers laying up in the bushes above the road. I made out like I didn't see 'em, but when I was by a piece I left my horse and circled around behind 'em. I figgered they wasn't there for no good.

"Well, sir, sheriff, they sure wasn't! I crep' up and listened. They was part of a band of about thirty cattle rustlers, and the west got too hot for 'em, so they come to do their rustlin' in New York State. They already rounded up some cows—none of these cows ain't branded here in the East, you see. All they got to do is put their own brand on 'em—well, they got three cows off a settler named—lemme see— named after some vegetable. I just can't remember—"

"Maybe 'twas Edgar Cucumber," said the sheriff. "He lives around here."

Freddy felt a little suspicious. He was supposed to be kidding the sheriff, the sheriff wasn't supposed to be kidding him.

"I got it!" he said. "Bean! That's the man. They got his cows and drove 'em up to Flint's —he's in with the gang. If you want to round 'em up, you better get you a posse and go up there. Shore be a feather in your cap pulling in thirty rustlers at one whack."

The prisoners looked at one another gloomily. The jail was pretty full now, and they had a nice time together. Thirty more guests would mean a lot of doubling up, and strangers, too. It would spoil a lot of their fun.

The sheriff polished his silver star on his sleeve and said: "Well, Mr. Peters, that's certainly news to me. But I got some news for you, too. There's a warrant out for your arrest. Let me see." He drew a paper from his pocket and pretended to read from it. "Snake Peters, long black hair, black moustache, little weasly eyes, large nose, has a very sly sneaky smile—yes, that fits. Face in repose—dirty. Eyebrows—none. Conversation—dull." He folded the paper. "I guess you're the Peters we want, all right."

Freddy saw that the sheriff knew who he was. It was very discouraging. He could fool lots of people with his disguises, but he had never yet been able to fool the sheriff. "Well," he said, "what's the charge against me?"

"Impersonating a pig," said the sheriff, and reached up suddenly and pulled Freddy out of the saddle. Then he snatched off the wig. "There you are, boys," he said to the prisoners;

here's our man. What'll we do with him?"

The prisoners all knew and liked Freddy, who often dropped in for a dish of ice cream and a game of croquet. "Stick him in solitary!" they said. "Bread and water." Red Mike said: "Maybe we'd better string him right up, sheriff. I'll give him a piece of my cake so he won't mind so much."

The idea of cake appealed to all of the prisoners, however, so they all went back in and Mike cut it and gave everybody a piece. Freddy told them his story, and at first they were all for going up to the ranch in a body and taking Mr. Flint apart. But the sheriff said no, he didn't think it would look well. "You know how people are," he said. "Always ready to find fault with us."

"It's my problem anyway," Freddy said. "If you can let me have a cell here for a few nights, sheriff, maybe I can think out something."

So they arranged it that way, and they had supper and after they had eaten up the rest of the cake for dessert, Red Mike said good-bye again and left. And this time he just sobbed right out loud when he went down the walk.

"I didn't know you could ride, Freddy," said

the sheriff. "Where did you learn?"

"My horse taught me," Freddy said.

"By George," said the sheriff, "that is the most sensible thing I ever heard of. Most people get a riding master to teach them. But you go right and hire the horse himself. How are you—pretty good?"

So before it got dark Freddy gave them an exhibition, and then he offered ten dollars to anybody who could stay on Cy ten seconds. Several of the prisoners were Texans who had got chased out of Texas and had come east to continue their professional activities, and naturally they thought they were pretty good riders. But Cy didn't even have to buck them off; he unseated them all with the same stumble and twist that he had used first on Mr. Flint. Afterwards they sat around on the lawn and had refreshments and talked.

They were sitting there when a strange procession came through the gate. First came the two dogs, Robert and Georgie, going sniff-sniff-sniff as they worked slowly up the drive. And after them came Bannister's car, chugging along in low, and sounding as if it, too, was sniffing out a trail, with Bannister at the wheel, and

Mrs. Wiggins peering anxiously over his shoulder.

The dogs, with eyes and noses on the ground, came sniff-sniff-sniff right up to Freddy, and then they raised their eyes and saw him. They began jumping up and down and yelping with delight, and Bannister piled out of the car and came up, and first he started very politely: "Mr. Frederick, sir, very happy to see you in good health"; and then he forgot his dignity and threw his arms around the pig and gave him a big hug.

"Will somebody get me *out* of this thing?" Mrs. Wiggins called. For they had left her in the car. So six of the prisoners ran out and lifted her out, and she came right up to Freddy and kissed him. I don't know if you have ever been kissed by a cow, but it is a large-scale operation. But Freddy didn't mind because he was very fond of Mrs. Wiggins.

"We thought you'd been shot, Freddy," she said, "because Old Whibley found your hat way up beyond the ranch, and it had bullet holes in it."

So Freddy explained that Mr. Bean was responsible for the bullet holes.

It is a large-scale operation.

"Well, my land," said the cow, "you certainly had us worried."

"And you can go right on worrying," Freddy said. "Flint's madder than ever at me now, and he'll shoot me if he gets a chance."

"Well, you got guns," said one of the prisoners. "Why don't you plug him first? Ambush him some night."

"This is why," Freddy said, and he pulled out his gun and pointed it at a big window which was about three feet behind him, and pulled the trigger.

"Hey, quit that!" the sheriff yelled, but he was too late to stop Freddy; and then he looked at the window, and there wasn't any hole in it, and he said: "Gosh sakes, you missed it!"

" 'Tain't possible to be as bad a shot as that," said a prisoner.

"It is for Freddy," said the sheriff. "I expect he could probably get to be famous as the worst shot in the world, if he set his mind to it. He's an awful smart pig."

So Freddy explained about the blanks, and told them the whole story.

"Well, you're welcome to stay here as long as you want to," said the sheriff.

"I thought nobody could stay in a jail unless he was a prisoner," said Mrs. Wiggins.

"Generally speakin', that's so," the sheriff said. "But we've made an exception before in Freddy's case. If there's any questions asked—well, we don't have to know he's Freddy, do we? He's a dangerous character—Snake Peters, claims his name is. Arrested for prancin' around town shootin' off guns and hollerin' and generally disturbing the public peace and creatin' a nuisance of himself. And if that ain't enough, I'll arrest him for wearin' that moustache. I never see such a thing in all my born days! Looks like two rat tails, tied together."

"It was thicker when I bought it," Freddy explained. "But I guess the hair wasn't fastened in very tight; it kind of sheds."

Cy, who had been out in the barn getting some oats, came around the corner of the jail. He stepped very carefully on the lawn, so as not to cut it up with his iron shoes. "Say, Freddy," he said, "that Cousin Augustus—I guess he had too much cake. He's out in the barn and he looks kind of greenish. Maybe you better come out—I ain't much of a hand nursing sick mice."

So Freddy and the sheriff went out. The

mouse was lying on his back on some hay in the manger, and moaning. When he saw his visitors he turned his head from them. "Go away," he said weakly. "Let me die in peace."

"No peace for the wicked, old boy," said Freddy cheerfully. "How about it, sheriff?"

"Kinda fretful, ain't he?" said the sheriff. He looked thoughtfully at the sufferer. "H'm, I know what's the matter. We've got just the thing for it—just the thing. Yes sir, just the thing for what ails you."

"Well, you needn't say it three times," said Cousin Augustus crossly. "Because I know what it is and I won't take any."

It isn't as easy as some people might imagine to give a mouse a dose of castor oil—even a mouse's dose, which is one drop. It took the sheriff and two of the prisoners to give it to Cousin Augustus. One prisoner held him, and the other held his nose, and the sheriff got the oil in his mouth and made him swallow it. And even then the prisoner named Looey got bitten in the thumb.

"I wonder how they give the animals medicine in these here zoos," said Looey when they were back on the lawn. "Lions and like that."

"Mr. Boomschmidt has a lot of animals in his circus," said Freddy. "The way he manages it, he's got a tame buzzard that really likes cod liver oil and such things. Old Boom gets the buzzard to smacking his beak over whatever nasty medicine he wants to give his animals, and then the animals are all so ashamed of being more scared of it than the buzzard is that they swallow it right down."

"Let's talk about something else," said the sheriff, and he swallowed uneasily himself several times. "I don't know but maybe I ate a mite too much of that cake myself."

So they talked about other things for a while, and then Bannister drove the dogs and Mrs. Wiggins back home, where the news that Freddy was alive and well was greeted with such a happy uproar that if Mr. Bean had been home, the animals would certainly have got a good talking to. It must have been midnight before they all quieted down and went to bed.

Chapter 16

For a couple of days Freddy stayed quietly at the jail. It was a nice place to visit. The sheriff was always thinking up little entertainments and parties to keep the prisoners contented and happy, and so there was never a dull moment. But Freddy was restless. It wasn't so much that he wanted to get back home, for he was, like most pigs, a sociable person, fond of games and banquets. But he felt that in the struggle between himself and Mr. Flint the man had come out ahead. Even though each time they came together Flint had got the worst of it, he still had the upper hand. He was free to move about the country, while Freddy was afraid to show so much as the tip of his curly tail in his own home territory.

So one day he saddled Cy and started out to do a little scouting. They were an odd-looking pair. Freddy wore his Snake Peters disguise; there were only about three hairs left on each side of the long moustache, which gave him a very sinister appearance. And the Easter egg tint was beginning to wear off Cy's coat, so that he looked, as the sheriff remarked, more like a leopard than a horse.

But Freddy's luck was out that day—at least the first part of the day. He was cantering along happily in the sunshine, the black hair of his wig flopping on his shoulders with the gentle rocking motion, when out from a patch of woods up a slope perhaps half a mile away rode two horsemen. Freddy recognized them easily —they were Mr. Flint and Jasper. He saw Jasper pull up sharply and point, and heard him shout; then the two spurred their horses to a gallop and came flying down towards him. Cy didn't wait for Freddy to say anything. He reared, pivoted, and set off towards Centerboro at a dead run.

They had been off the road, riding through some abandoned hill pastures, several miles north of town. But there was no use taking to the road. On level ground, Mr. Flint's horse would overhaul them in another mile. The only hope of escape was to hide in a patch of woods, or to try to slow up the pursuit in rough country, where Flint's horse would be at a disadvantage. There was a marshy stretch below them, and Cy headed for that.

Cy went slowly in the wet ground, jumping carefully from one clump of dry grass to another. At first the men overhauled them rapidly, but once the horses got into the swampy piece they slowed down, and although Flint got close enough to throw two or three rapid shots after the fugitive, when he got through to solid ground again he had lost half a mile.

And the chase went on. It was rather like playing Follow The Leader. Cy picked the toughest going and the others had to follow. He was getting farther and farther ahead, and Freddy began to think that they might escape.

The jail, he felt, was the only safe place, and Cy agreed that they should do their best to reach it. But pretty soon they began to get close to town, and with so many gardens and cultivated fields and wire fences, they could no longer go cross country. Cy cut down to the road, which soon became a street, and then, although Jasper had fallen way behind, Mr. Flint came up fast. Freddy knew that he could never reach the jail, which was on the other side of town.

The people living on upper Main Street heard a rattle of hoofs and the bang of a six-gun, and they ran to their doors. Down the street, running like a scared rabbit, came a queer spotty-looking pony, and on his back crouched a small but wild looking desperado, with long black hair that streamed behind him. And close on his heels came a grim sour-faced cowboy, brandishing a big Colt .45, and lashing his horse with a heavy quirt. Judge Willey came to his window, looked out, said: "H'm, taking movies, I expect," and pulled down the shade. Old Mrs. Peppercorn was out mopping her front porch. She ran down to the gate and waved her mop as Freddy came by, and called: "Ride 'em, cowboy!" And then she looked again and thought: "Why that's my friend, Freddy!" So when Mr. Flint came opposite her, she swung the mop around her head and let it fly at him.

She was a quick-witted old lady, but not a very good shot. The mop whirled across in front of Mr. Flint, and the handle rapped his horse smartly on the nose; but the mop went right on across the street, and the long trail of wet rags went smack! against the front parlor window of Mrs. Lafayette Bingle. As Mrs. Bingle was looking out of the window at the time, it made her jump; and that made her mad; and what made her madder was that she had just washed that window that morning, and now it was all dirty again. She came out and told Mrs. Peppercorn what she thought of her. So that made Mrs. Peppercorn mad, and *she* told Mrs. Bingle what *she* thought of *her*. It was the beginning of a feud between Mrs. Peppercorn and Mrs. Bingle that lasted for a long, long time.

But in the meantime Freddy had gained a little. The rap from the mop handle had naturally surprised Mr. Flint's horse, and he reared and bucked for a minute, and Mr.

Flint yelled at him and whacked him with the quirt as if he was beating a carpet, so he started again. By that time Freddy had got down into the shopping section of Main Street. He had to go slower here, weaving in and out among the cars; and indeed he practically stopped all traffic, for the people on the sidewalks crowded to the curb to stare at him. Some of them recognized him as the Snake Peters who had been at the rodeo, but many just stared because they had never seen anything like him before.

But he was being overtaken rapidly. Mr. Flint wasn't as careful as Freddy, and he drove his horse right through the people. He knocked over two little boys, and he slashed savagely at Dr. Winterbottom, who didn't get out of the way quickly enough. And he deliberately rode down a Mr. Abraham Winkus, who didn't even live in Centerboro but had come there to visit his married stepdaughter who ran a beauty shop, a Mrs. Nellie Champoux. Fortunately Mr. Winkus was tough, and he wasn't hurt much. He only got a broken arm.

Freddy didn't think Mr. Flint would dare shoot at him with such a lot of people around, but he saw that the man was in a terrific rage, and he decided he had better not take a chance. As he passed Beller & Rohr's radio and jewelry shop, he saw Mr. Beller looking out of the door, and he shouted to him to phone the sheriff, but Mr. Beller didn't hear him. Then he pulled Cy up sharply so that the pony skidded to a stop right in front of the Busy Bee Department Store, threw himself out of the saddle, and darted in through the revolving door.

A number of sales had been announced for that day in the Busy Bee, and the store was crowded. Very few people noticed Freddy at first, for their eyes were searching for bargains, and they didn't look at anything but what was displayed on the counters. A dozen cannibals with spears and rings in their noses could walk through the average bargain day crowd in a department store and nobody would ever see them. Freddy slipped through and took the elevator to the second floor.

And this, I guess, was where he made a mistake. For there were no bargains displayed on this floor, which was given up mostly to women's suits, coats and dresses. And people began to look. They began to crowd around him. And a young lady pushed through and said: "Excuse me, sir, is there something I can show you?"

"You can show me the back stairs, if you will be so kind," Freddy said.

She was a very haughty young lady with hair so neat that it looked as if it was made out of tin and painted, and she drew herself up and said: "I don't know what you mean, I'm shaw!"

Freddy really didn't mean to mimic her, but you know how it is when someone has a funny way of talking, and you find yourself doing the same thing before you know it. "Well, I'm shaw you do, miss," he said. "I'm shaw you know where the back staws aw."

She gave him a very dirty look, and standing on tiptoes, stared over the heads of the crowd and called: "Mr. Metacarpus!"

Mr. Metacarpus was the manager of the store. He had a big moustache which hung down over his mouth, and he drew it in and then blew it out again before he said anything. Now he came bustling up. "Yes, Miss Jones? No trouble here, I hope?"

"Perhaps you can take care of this—this gentleman," she said. "He has insulted me."

"Oh, rats!" said Freddy. "I just asked where the stairs were."

"Rats, is it?" Miss Jones drew herself up and glared. "The eye-dawcity!" And she flounced off.

Mr. Metacarpus blew out his moustache. "I don't think there is anything on this floor that would interest you, sir," he said. "May I show you to the sporting goods department?"

"I don't know why the sporting goods department would want to have me shown to them," Freddy said. He heard a vague distant sound of shouting that seemed to come from the floor below. Mr. Flint was probably tearing the store to pieces looking for him. "Haven't you got any back stairs to this place?"

"Stairs?" said Mr. Metacarpus, looking puzzled. "I'm sorry, sir, we have only ladies' wear up here: coats and suits, dresses; cosmetics over there in Aisle F—"

"I don't want to *buy* stairs, Metacarpus," said Freddy angrily. "I want you to put 'em *under* me, so I can go down 'em. There's a man downstairs chasing me with a gun, and—" He broke off as the elevator door opened with a clang and Mr. Flint's voice shouted: "Where is he? Where's that pig?"

The shoppers had crowded so close around

Freddy that he couldn't push through them. He whipped out his gun and swung it in a half circle. "Stand back!" he shouted, and as they shrieked and melted away from him he darted down one aisle, up another, then ducked behind a counter. He looked around cautiously. He was behind the perfumery counter, and there was no one there but him. The girl in charge had run out to see what the excitement was.

Mr. Flint had herded the shoppers and Mr. Metacarpus and most of the salespeople into a corner at the point of his gun, and was making a systematic search. Freddy knew that he would certainly be caught. He thought: "If I only had time to put on one of those dresses and pretend to be a salesgirl! Maybe I could sell Mr. Flint a bottle of perfumery." But there was no time for such thoughts. He had to do something. His gun, loaded with blanks, was worse than useless. Even his water pistol was empty. Yet a good squirt of water at the right moment might give him a chance to run. But there wasn't any water.

Then he saw the big bottle of perfume just above him on the counter. He took it down and uncorked it. It was a heavy, sweet perfume; a very little bit of it might have been all right, but a lot of it together was pretty sickening. Freddy sniffed, said: "Whew! Gosh!" and started to put it back. Then he changed his mind. He filled the water pistol full.

Mr. Flint was searching the floor, counter by counter. Mr. Metacarpus stood back wringing his hands and puffing unhappily through his moustache. Behind him, twenty or more women looked on fearfully as the rancher threw down racks of dresses, poked under shelves and counters, and called on Freddy to come out and fight like a man.

It was taking Mr. Flint some time. Freddy found some hairpins and hurriedly pinned up the long black hair into a knot on top of his head. He yanked off the rat-tail moustache and rouged his cheeks, and made an enormous Cupid's bow mouth for himself with lipstick, and even put on some eye shadow, making his little pig's eyes look much larger. He had to work in the dark back of the counter, and he used whichever lipstick and rouge came first to hand, but when he looked at himself in one of the little compact mirrors he almost fainted.

"Oh, my gracious!" he said. "If Mr. Bean saw me now he'd throw me off the farm!" He didn't really look much like a salesgirl. But he certainly didn't look like a pig.

However, it was his only chance. He found a scarf under the counter and put it over his shoulders, covering up the cowboy shirt. And then, as Mr. Flint turned into Aisle F, he stood up behind the counter, and with an inviting smile on his big lipsticked mouth—and one of the women said afterwards that he looked like a cannibal chief inviting a missionary to step into the stewpot—he said: "Could I interest you in our newest French perfume, sir? The latest thing from Paris." He pushed the bottle forward.

Mr. Flint checked and swung round to face the pig. And then he jumped back with a sort of yelp, for Freddy was certainly the most terrible looking salesgirl that had ever appeared behind a counter.

But Freddy pulled out the water pistol and leaned forward. "May I put just a dab on your pocket handkerchief, sir? I'm sure you'll find it refreshing." And he squirted the entire contents of the pistol into the man's face.

Mr. Flint yelped again—with pain this time, for the perfume had gone into his eyes. He dropped his pistols and sputtered and danced about, pawing at his face, which was streaming with perfumery. Freddy jumped the counter, snatched up the guns, and then waited, holding them on Flint, till the man had cleared his eyes so he could see.

"Turn your back to me, Flint," he commanded. "Yes, it's me—Freddy. Stick up your hands and turn your back." And when Mr. Flint had done so, he quickly refilled the water pistol and deliberately squirted it onto the rancher's clothing. Then he refilled it once more, tucked it into his holster, picked up the gun he had laid down, and made his captive walk over to the elevator.

The crowd of onlookers shrank back at the sight of the big Colt revolvers, and several of them grew quite faint—though Freddy thought it was as much at the smell of the perfume as any idea of danger. Of course he hadn't really got a good look at himself in a mirror, or he would have known better what had terrorized them. As he passed Mr. Metacarpus, he said: "You can charge that bottle of perfumery to

He squirted the entire contents of the pistol into the man's face.

me, Frederick Bean, Mr. Metacarpus. I guess you know me."

Mr. Metacarpus bowed and puffed his moustache.

Freddy herded his prisoner down in the elevator and out between rows of gasping and sniffing shoppers, to the street. There, before he told Mr. Flint to get on his horse, he took his rope and tossed a loop over the man's shoulders, pulled it tight, and hitched the free end around his saddle horn. Flint's pony was faster than Cy; he had no intention of letting the rancher escape until he had finished with him.

About an hour later, just as the dudes were coming out from dinner, Freddy and Mr. Flint rode up to the ranch house. Freddy fired a shot in the air, and immediately they were surrounded. He kept one gun on the raging Flint, and with the other covered Jasper and Slim, who looked as if they might be going to attempt a rescue.

"You two boys," he said—"don't start anything. I'm not going to hurt your boss—just going to make a little speech and let him go. And while I'm not much of a shot, these bullets make you kind of jump if they do hit you.

"Now, ladies and gentlemen," he went on, "Mr. Flint, here, is awful mad at me, and he claimed he was going to shoot me on sight. I admit I was scared. I'm not any hero. Besides, I haven't got anything but a water pistol and a gun with blanks in it."

"But you shot those cans the other night," said one of the dudes.

"I didn't hit the cans," Freddy said. "It was just a trick. I'll show you some time how it was done."

"What's the matter with you, Jasper?" Mr. Flint called angrily. "You and Slim want to get fired? Are you going to stand there and let this fat monkey make a fool of me?"

"Looks like that was done before you rode up here, boss," Jasper drawled. "Or maybe I ought to say it *smells* like it. You been to a beauty parlor or somethin'?"

"Yes, what *is* that awful smell?" said Mrs. Balloway. She stepped forward, sniffing. "Why I do believe—why, it's Mr. Flint!"

Some of the dudes began to giggle, but Freddy said: "Please! Let me finish. Well, Mr. Flint threatened me and I ran away and hid. I guess you know most of the story. I don't like

Mr. Flint. I had to buy this pony from him because he would have beaten it to death if I hadn't. He tried to rob our bank, but my friends drove him off. There's a lot of other things, too, but I won't go into them. It came down to a straight fight between him and me—him with these two guns I'm holding on him, and me with a revolver loaded with blanks, and a water pistol. Well, he caught up with me today. And all I want to say is: I got the drop on him. I shot him with my water pistol before he could draw and shoot. And now, my friends, I'm going to shoot him again, just for good measure." He tucked one gun in his belt, drew the water pistol, and squirted its contents over both Flint and his pony.

For a minute there was silence, as the rank sweet reek of the perfume filled the hot noon air. Then Jasper began to laugh. It was like touching off a pack of firecrackers; the laugh spread; there were at first a few isolated giggles and hoots, and then the whole crowd was roaring. They yelled and shouted, pounded one another on the backs, and gasped and got red in the face and still went on laughing until they had to lie down on the ground. Through it all

Freddy and Mr. Flint sat on their horses without moving.

At last when the crowd was too weak to make any more noise, Freddy said: "O K, Flint; you can get down."

So Mr. Flint dismounted and started into the ranch house. But Jasper said: "Hey, keep out of the house. These folks don't want to have it all smelled up so they can't live in it."

"You're fired," said Mr. Flint.

"I fired myself ten minutes ago," said the cowboy. "A boss that goes out with two six-guns and gets shot up with a water pistol ain't any boss I can work for. Even if he comes back smellin' sweeter'n a greenhouse full of posies."

"Me too," said Slim. "You shore are the sweetest smellin' buckaroo ever decorated this ranch. Folks ought to put you in a vase and set you on the piano."

Flint glared at them a moment. "O K," he said at last; "you're fired yourselves. But come over here a minute."

So they went over close to him and held their noses while he whispered to them for a time. At first they looked doubtful, but then they began nodding their heads, and pretty soon Mr.

Flint walked over to one of the buildings where he would be out of sight and out of smelling range of the dudes. And Slim went into the house.

Jasper spoke to the crowd. "Folks," he said, "Cal's quit. We was his partners in the ranch, but he was the boss. But now he's quit and we're running the place. Slim's packin' his stuff for him, and when he rides out of here he won't come back."

And that was the way it worked out. Mr. Flint had the sense to realize that if he stayed on, the dudes would giggle and laugh at him every time they saw him. He couldn't face their ridicule; he had not only made a fool of himself, he had made a perfumed fool of himself.

And indeed his troubles pursued him as he rode on west. For the perfume wouldn't come off, no matter how much he scrubbed, and sent his clothes to the dry cleaner's. Clerks in hotels where he engaged a room for the night sniffed disgustedly, and people in restaurants got up and moved away from him. There were even pieces in the local papers of towns he stopped in—all about the mysterious Perfumed Cowboy. But he never came back to the ranch.

Freddy rode back home, and that night there was a big party in the cow barn in his honor. There were refreshments, and speeches—one by Charles lasted an hour and a half—and there was dancing, and the singing of some of the cowboy songs Freddy had written. The Horrible Ten put on a splendid floor show, which a visiting spaniel, who had traveled a good deal, said was the equal of anything he had seen in New York.

Freddy made a speech, too. He tried to be modest, but it is hard to be modest when you are the hero of the occasion, and I guess he did pat himself on the back quite a lot. But one thing he said was pretty good. Mac, the wildcat, wanted to know why he hadn't just shot Mr. Flint and got it over quick.

Freddy said: "There are two ways of getting rid of people: one way is by shooting them; the other way is by making them look ridiculous. I didn't want to shoot Mr. Flint, even though he wanted to shoot me. But squirting that perfume over him made everybody laugh at him, and he couldn't stand that. That was the easiest way to get rid of him."

Of course, like most reasons people have for

the things they do, I think Freddy made it up afterwards. At the time he wasn't thinking of making people laugh at Flint; he just wanted to stop the man from shooting him. But there is a lot of truth in what he said, just the same.

The party was at its height, and Mrs. Wiggins and Bill, the goat, were trying to do an apache dance together—it wasn't very good, but it was funny all right—when one of the Horrible Ten announced that he thought he heard the Beans driving into the barnyard.

"Good land of mercy!" said Mrs. Wiggins. "It's after eleven! Get to bed, animals. Lights out!" In one minute the barn was dark and silent.

Mr. Bean unhitched Hank and shook some hay down into his manger, and he was following Mrs. Bean into the house when he saw Freddy crossing the barnyard. The pig had been the last to leave.

"Here, you!" he called, and Freddy came across to him. "Oh, it's you," he said. "Well, I expect you've been looking for us before this. Didn't expect to stay so long. But Aunt Effie, she has buckwheat cakes every morning. And you know how it is when the cakes and the butter and the syrup don't come out even. You go on eatin' till they do. Well, they didn't come out even till this mornin'. So then we got in the buggy and came home." He paused. "Don't know why I'm explainin' this to you," he said. "Everything been quiet at home, here?"

"Very quiet," said Freddy.

"No trouble? Nothing exciting happen?"

"No, sir, very peaceful time we all had."

"Good!" said Mr. Bean, and he whacked Freddy on the back and went on to the house.